Those Who Dwell Below

Aviaq Johnston

Illustrations by

Toma Feizo Gas

INHABIT
MEDIA

Published by Inhabit Media Inc.
www.inhabitmedia.com

Inhabit Media Inc. (Iqaluit), P.O. Box 11125, Iqaluit, Nunavut, X0A 1H0
(Toronto), 191 Eglinton Avenue East, Suite 310, Toronto, Ontario, M4P 1K1

Design and layout copyright © 2019 Inhabit Media Inc.
Text copyright © 2019 by Aviaq Johnston
Illustrations by Toma Feizo Gas copyright © 2019 Inhabit Media Inc.

Editors: Neil Christopher and Kelly Ward
Art director: Danny Christopher

We acknowledge the support of the Canada Council for the Arts for our
publishing program.

This project was made possible in part by the Government of Canada.

Printed in Canada

Library and Archives Canada Cataloguing in Publication

Title: Those who dwell below / Aviaq Johnston ; illustrations by Toma Feizo Gas.
Names: Johnston, Aviaq, author. | Gas, Toma Feizo, 1979- illustrator.
Identifiers: Canadiana 20190106131 | ISBN 9781772272352 (softcover)
Classification: LCC PS8619.O4848 T56 2019 | DDC jC813/.6—dc23

We do not believe. We fear.

 ～ **Aua** ～

This book is dedicated to Alannah, nerd-lakaujaq and maqi-ears. Ain.

1

The Storyteller

E ach block of snow was cut with excellent precision. With sweat dripping from their brows, the men of the village sliced their sharp knives through the hard snow with patience, with meticulousness, until they had built an *iglu*. Then another. And two more. All large enough for an average family to live in comfortably. Finally, they began to build a *qaggiq*, an iglu large enough to encompass all the people of the village. They connected the sturdy blocks of snow together, fastening them to four *igluit* used as a base.

Slowly, the snow house was built. The men took turns, some cutting the blocks, some stacking them upon the other blocks. Women came and brought them water and freshly caught fish to eat when they needed a break. Children knew to stay outside, away from the working men, afraid they might distract them—or worse, they might be asked to help.

As the last of the blocks was being set up, a young man entered the almost-finished qaggiq, holding an ivory snow knife in hand. He gripped it firmly, as if it were a part of his own body. Across the chest of his caribou-skin parka was a large necklace with the bones of a fox displayed, the skull as its centrepiece. He wore an easy-going smile on his lips, but behind his eyes there was an untold story. A story he would tell tonight.

The men in the qaggiq stopped their work and greeted the young man. "*Piturniirngai*," they said. "Hello, Piturniq."

"*Ai*," he said, not quite used to the sign of respect that greeting implied from men older and more experienced than he.

They moved out of the way and watched the young man cut out several blocks on his own. He moved them to the centre of the qaggiq and looked up. The top of the qaggiq was much too high for him to reach. The young man scratched his head and looked at the men who surrounded him.

He smiled, embarrassed. "I need some help."

Another man, not much older than him, offered, "You can stand on my back."

The young man hesitated. He was wary of this man, Ijiraq, but he soon accepted the offer. As the soon-to-be new leader and shaman of the village, he knew he had to put aside his differences. Ijiraq crouched down on all fours, and Piturniq balanced on his back. Piturniq's brother Natsivaq passed him the blocks of snow, and one by one, the iglu came closer to completion.

Once he secured the last block and cut out a space for the air and heat to escape, Piturniq jumped from Ijiraq's back and helped him stand. "*Qujannamiik*," he said. "Thank you, Ijiraq."

Ijiraq raised his eyebrows to acknowledge Pitu's thanks and left without another word. As the last of the men began to leave, giving one last admiring look at their hard work, Pitu was left alone with Natsivaq.

"Well, you were nice to him," Natsivaq observed.

"It was hard," Pitu admitted, "but he's been nothing but kind since I came back. It would be foolish for me to keep ignoring him."

"Let's go take a nap," Natsivaq suggested. "You'll need your energy for tonight, little brother."

They left the qaggiq. Natsivaq went to his family and ate some frozen seal liver before he lay down on the polar bear–hide bedding. Piturniq went to his own iglu, only big enough for himself. He lit the lamp by rubbing stone and flint, sparking the seal blubber to life. Removing his parka, Piturniq lay on the softness of the caribou hide he used as bedding. Interspersed upon his bed were the pelts of foxes, which he'd trapped in order to make his connection to his *tuurngaq*, his spiritual companion, stronger.

As he shut his eyes, Piturniq did not see the familiar fox shape of Tiri, his ever-present spirit guide, but only the beauty of the girl he had lost. He knew that all that was separating them was the snow walls of their igluit, and the eyes of the people in the village, and the arms of her husband, Ijiraq.

He tried to sleep, but found he was not tired.

The qaggiq was dimly lit. The people of the village all sat against the walls on benches made of snow. The space in the middle was left wide and open, welcoming to anyone who may have a story to share or a game to play. For once, the children were silent, sitting in the laps of their parents, aunts, uncles, siblings, or grandparents. The whole village watched quietly as their shaman walked into the iglu.

In the centre of the qaggiq stood Piturniq, clutching a large drum in his hands. He'd caught the caribou himself, harvested it without help. He had prepared and stretched the skin, fashioned it upon the drum frame he'd made from the flexible baleen of a bowhead whale. He'd made a *katuut*, a drum beater, from the bone of the caribou's leg, wrapping it in a bit of fur to cushion his hand and to make the sound as it struck the drum more pleasant.

Piturniq had never told a story at a celebration before, and to do so as a shaman during Qaggiq, the most joyous gathering of all, was another responsibility altogether. Qaggiq was more than just the giant iglu they were in; it was the name of the celebration itself, the gathering itself. It was the anticipation of the approaching spring, the end of the dark winter. Pitu took a deep breath. He'd only ever seen one other shaman speak about his own tale prior to this. Nerves spread throughout his body. His stomach ached.

"I found myself lost on the ice," he began, quietly, nervously. "My dog team disappeared, and the only tools I had were a harpoon and my beloved snow knife."

The crowd chuckled slightly at his loving words about the knife.

"I knew I was far from home," he continued, "but I heard the cry of a woman, so I went to her to see if I could help her, or if she could help me."

The onlookers were silent.

"I saw the woman, far away, with two others." His voice grew stronger the longer he spoke. "And I ran toward them, happy that I did not have to travel too long to find help . . . but these were not women."

The women of the crowd gasped, while the men looked confused.

"As they revealed themselves to me, I saw their scaly skin, their hollow cheeks and sharp teeth," he said. "*Qallupilluit*, searching for new children to prey on!"

Children buried themselves into the embrace of their loved ones.

"Once they saw me, they attacked!" Pitu continued. "They slashed into my parka with their sharp nails, and we fought until I killed the leader. The others fled into the field of ice. I left the body of the qallupilluq to the wilds of the spirit world."

The crowd whooped and clapped, but they didn't know the most terrible part of the story. He neglected to talk about the tiny boy he'd found, blue and frozen in the qallupilluq's *amauti*, or the little girl he'd found in there, too, in the midst of transformation from human to creature. He fought back the pain he remembered. He fought the memory of the girl refusing his help.

"But as I left the qallupilluq behind, I did not know that a monstrous black wolf stalked me," Pitu continued shakily. "For days, the wolf followed me with its pack, until finally they caught me, and we fought. They were made of darkness and shadows, but I fought them off.

"I was so tired, and I was suffering from deep scratches left by the wolves. Yet I was no closer to the end of my journey. Only a short while later, another visitor came. A lonesome giant, desperate to find a companion. Her name was Inukpak, and she stole me away to her camp in the mountains of the spirit world, where she had caribou, wolves, and polar bears as pets. She was adding me to her collection.

"It was only a matter of time before those dark wolves found me again. Inukpak left the camp to search for more food for her animals, and the wolves surrounded the camp and took me away." Pitu lowered his sealskin boot and lifted the leg of his pants to show an ugly black scar left by the wolf's jaws.

"I don't know how long or how far away they carried me. After one last fight against the wolves, they left me to die. But again, my journey was not yet over. I thought I had died, but I awoke in a tent with an elder named Taktuq, a shaman of great power and little patience. He healed me, and then he taught me the ways of the shamans and spirits. We worked together until there was little else to learn. Then we started the journey home.

"But still, those wolves stalked me. We could not simply leave the sanctuary of our camp, which was protected from the spirits. Taktuq called upon a guide, the spirits that run across our dark winter skies. The northern lights. We ran across stretches of land so massive it was almost incomprehensible. Still, the wolves caught up to us, and our fight with them was bloody and painful.

"We were saved by the giant. Inukpak came to our aid, with her polar bears coming to fight the wolves. The northern lights and I kept running, until finally we reached the place where the whole journey had begun. The crack in the ice where I had met the qallupilluit."

Pitu coughed, his mouth dry from speaking and the memory of all that had happened. Still he refrained from telling all the details. They did not need to know that the wolf had been Taktuq's tuurngaq, or that he didn't know whether Inukpak had survived. He did not tell them about his father's spirit being among those who run in the sky. He felt these details were his to keep.

"The qallupilluit had been waiting for my return," Pitu said. "But I had learned a lot over the time I spent in the spirit world, and I had grown stronger. The qallupilluit fought until the large black wolf caught up. They worked together, and yet again, I thought that I was going to die.

"But my journey did not end there. No." Pitu looked down to his feet, remembering what Taktuq had done next to ensure Pitu's survival. "Taktuq, my great friend, fought the wolf alone. He sacrificed himself so that I could return. He killed the wolf, and in turn, the wolf killed him."

As he ended his story, Pitu began his drumming. Steadily he struck the baleen frame of his drum. In a circle, he danced in imitation of a caribou. The crowd watched in silence, mesmerized by his performance. A woman, Pitu's mother, chanted the words of a song she'd made for him—not one of darkness or turmoil, but a song of light. As she sang, the sun rose a sliver above the horizon for the first time since it had last set at the long-ago arrival of winter. A hunter burst into the iglu just as the song and drumming ended, calling excitedly, "The sun has returned!"

The villagers left the qaggiq in haste, wanting to catch a glimpse of the sun. It barely peeked over the edge of the horizon, but it was there, filling them with hope. Pitu gazed at the light, feeling it burn a line across his sight. He felt a hand playfully swipe across his arm in passing, and he blinked toward the person who'd touched him. It was Saima, a sheepish grin across her face that didn't melt away the hint of sadness within her eyes. He only knew because his own eyes reflected the same sadness. He smiled back at her and turned his gaze back to the sun.

It was the first sunrise in months, and with it came the hope for a plentiful season of health and happiness.

2

Tagaaq

Pitu entered his mentor's iglu, finding the elder sitting with his legs stretched out before him. The elder was alone, his wife gone to fetch water or visit her grandchildren. Tagaaq carved a shape into soapstone with a shard of bone. He looked up as Pitu entered and gave him a toothy grin.

It was hard to believe how much Tagaaq had aged in the time since Pitu was found and returned from the spirit world. His hair had begun to fall out, and the strands that remained were whiter than the snow. The wrinkles on his face had deepened, and the elder never seemed able to catch his breath anymore.

"*Ullaakkut*," Tagaaq said. "Good morning, Piturniq. Come, sit down."

"Ullaakkut," Pitu replied. He took his seat next to Tagaaq on the bedding. Remembering the carving Tagaaq had made for him months ago—a stone hunter just big enough to fit in the palm of his hand—he asked, "What are you making?"

"Something for my wife to remember me by," Tagaaq answered, his regular humour leaving his voice, replaced with serious reflection. "I fear I don't have much longer on this earth. My mother's spirit has faded, and her strength no longer flows through me."

Pitu felt the heaviness of Tagaaq's words. The spirit of Tagaaq's mother had watched over the camp for decades, but as Pitu grew stronger as a shaman, she was no longer needed. A part of him couldn't help but feel somewhat guilty, though he knew that her spirit wouldn't have been able to look after them forever. Pitu did not reply to Tagaaq.

Pitu's silence was no worry to the elder. He resumed his carving and continued to talk, returning to his normal self. "You were quite good last night, you know?" Tagaaq said. "With your story, jumping at the children to be scary. And your drumming is quite amazing."

"Thank you," Pitu said.

"You really remind me of Taktuq when I first met him," Tagaaq added. "He was nervous, too, when he was younger, but his people loved him."

"Hopefully I don't follow Taktuq's path."

"Yes, yes," Tagaaq said, blowing hard to remove carving dust from the figure. He held it up for Pitu to see. "What do you think? Does it look like me?"

The carving was oval-shaped and depicted a man's face. A straight line made the mouth of the figure, and two more lines made the eyes. Two indented holes made the nostrils, and framing the whole face were lines to make up the texture of a fur-lined hood. Despite the simplicity of the design, it was a remarkable likeness of the old man.

"It does," Pitu said.

"I would suggest a walk to the lake close by for a lesson, but I am feeling weak today," Tagaaq said. The elder stretched his arms and back. Pitu could hear his joints cracking. "How are you feeling today, Piturniq?"

Pitu shrugged. Every lesson started off with this question, and Pitu had great trouble trying to answer it accurately. He still mourned for Taktuq, even though he knew that his reluctant friend was in a happier place, running in the sky. Pitu was still upset about losing Saima to another man. Then there were the other things to think of—his mother's health, his sister's maturity that would soon lead to marriage, and, most perplexing of all, his little brother's drastic change from a rowdy child to a boy wanting to take on more responsibility. Finally, Pitu answered, "I'm feeling tired."

"You have a lot on your mind, young shaman," Tagaaq said. "Your absence changed things in our community."

"Was I gone for so long?" Pitu asked. "It felt like ages when I was on the other side, but time moves differently in the spirit world. I didn't think I'd lose so many things . . . so many people . . . while I was gone."

It wasn't just the loss of Taktuq and Saima. His little brother, Atiq, had lost his childhood, having had to take on more responsibility in anticipation of losing Pitu again. His little sister, Arnaapik, was getting closer and closer to marriage and caring for a family of her own. Among his friends, Pitu felt alone, his youth lost. Now he held great power and status in the village. No one wanted to interact with him, afraid to become the audience of the spirits, to experience the supernatural world.

Pitu could remember the fear of the spirits he had felt before he became a shaman. It was nothing compared to the constant fear he had now, but it had seemed all-encompassing before. Throughout his childhood, Pitu's parents and older siblings often told him of all the respect he needed to have for the spirits, to avoid angering them. This was ingrained into each child as they grew.

Day-to-day life in the harsh reality of the world was a precarious thing, subject to the whims of those who cannot be seen. If one failed to pay respect to the spirits, there would be backlash: starvation, bad weather, illness, death. He couldn't blame the villagers for their avoidance; he'd have done the same thing. There was an infinitesimal separation between the world of humans and the world of spirits, and often they intricately overlapped.

"We have this conversation every day, my friend," Tagaaq said. "It seems you are still thinking that things will go back to the way they were before you left, but it will never be the same. *You* have changed. The longer you mourn the past, the longer it will take for things to move forward."

It was true that they had been carrying on this conversation for weeks now. Pitu wondered endlessly when things would go back to normal, when Atiq would be restless and rowdy, when people wouldn't look at Pitu with fear and respect in their eyes, when the marriage between Saima and Ijiraq would be cancelled.

He'd been putting off talking about Saima with Tagaaq. But each day brought more discomfort, more pain. Pitu would see Saima standing close to Ijiraq, he'd run into Saima's parents and see their shame. It was they who had suggested the marriage, assuming that Pitu was dead. Now, after the private glance he'd shared with Saima last night, he wanted to ask Tagaaq a question.

"Why wouldn't you let Saima and I get married before I left?"

Tagaaq hung his head, looking down at the hard-packed snow floor. Pitu's heartbeat quickened, recognizing that look as shame. He didn't carry on with all the words that banged around in his head. *If you'd allowed our marriage, I would be happy right now. If you'd allowed our marriage, my life wouldn't have changed so much.*

Tagaaq, still looking down, spoke. "It is a part of your path, Piturniq. You will understand all that I've done when you are ready."

Pitu shook his head out of frustration, felt his face burning. He respected Tagaaq far too much to burst out in anger, as he had with Taktuq, but a part of him wanted to do something, to say more, to ask for a full answer for once.

The elder needed no prompting, it seemed. Tagaaq continued, "You are not ready, Piturniq. There are great forces within the world that are telling me so.

If you listen, you will hear their message. You will face far more danger soon. It is unclear if you will be strong enough to survive."

The words were a shock to Piturniq. He could feel that something was coming, another storm he'd have to weather. He didn't think it had anything to do with readiness. "What does that have to do with my relationship with Saima?" Pitu asked.

"Hold on to your questions of her, Piturniq," Tagaaq replied, sharper than usual. "You must remember that I've lost a great deal of my connection to the wind. The last thing I remember them telling me is that you will meet a great power that will answer your questions. When the moment comes, you will know."

Pitu found it in himself to stop asking about her. Changing the subject, he asked, "How must I prepare for the coming danger, Uncle?"

"Lots of practice," Tagaaq said with sarcasm. "Right now, focus your energies on your little brother. He needs you. I have a feeling that you won't have to chase whatever trials you must face. They will come to find you."

"I'm planning to take Atiq hunting soon," Pitu acknowledged.

"Hmm," Tagaaq said. "That's a good idea."

They sat in silence, unsure how to move forward. Pitu had come for a lesson, but Tagaaq had lost too much of his spirit. The elder had become short-tempered, losing the humour he'd found in every part of life. Now, he was easily tired. Tagaaq sighed. "I will tell you a story, Piturniq. A short one for today."

Pitu settled more comfortably.

"There is a place in the spirit world called *Nagliktaujut Nunangat*," Tagaaq said, "The place where the Naglitaujuit live. It is a place where the spirits of those who were neglected and abused are welcomed, loved, and healed.

"In this place, souls filled with pain and great sorrow collect." Tagaaq coughed. "It is in a part of the spirit world that is almost impossible to navigate, the land of the dead. You see, those who die in peace, they are placed with the northern lights; they are placed in the sky to carry on in joy and celebration for eternity, never tiring and never needing.

"But not everyone dies at peace. In fact, only the smallest number of people leave us when they are ready to." Tagaaq coughed again. Pitu picked up a cup made from tightly sewn sealskin and filled it from a larger sealskin bucket of melted ice water. He handed the water to Tagaaq, who took a long sip.

Once his voice returned, less hoarse than before, Tagaaq continued. "All those lost souls, they must find another place to carry on once they leave us. They must find a place to move forward from.

"Sometimes, those souls are in such turmoil; their lives have been too harsh, they have faced too much hurt, too much pain to find their own way. That is why Nagliktaujut Nunangat exists. They become a *Nagliktaujuq*, one who is shown pity for their unloved life. For they did not know love or safety when they were alive, but the spirits of the afterworld ensure that they know it from then on.

"Angugaattiaq, my mother, would often travel the spirit world as a *qupanuaq*, a snow bunting. You see, someday you will learn to transform into the same shape as your tuurngaq, as many shamans do.

"My mother would be guided by her tuurngaq throughout our world and the spirit world with great care. She could see much more when she was in the spirit world, though she was still blind as she was in life. One time, her tuurngaq took her to Nagliktaujut Nunangat at a time our village was being led by a man with many troubles. He would take his troubles out on his family and on others, but no one did anything to stop this treatment, though everyone knew it was happening.

"My mother's tuurngaq brought her to Nagliktaujut Nunangat to show her what happens to those who suffer from abuse and neglect.

"She found a land full of bittersweetness. Since she was blind, her tuurngaq would whisper to her what she could not see. Faceless spirits would be awakened by caretakers, their faces no longer unseen. These spirits would be given attention, given the care they needed and the praise they craved. The spirits ate it up. It was their life force . . . then they would become faceless again.

"You see, those spirits would learn to be loved, to feel acceptance, to feel the care they so desperately deserved, but their souls would remain broken. They could never find a way to move on from the abuse and pain they had known so well in their lives.

"My mother returned to her home, to our village, and she stopped that horrible man from leading our people. She told him how he would live in the next life, for she knew that he was in some way just as broken as the Naglitaujuit. No one abuses for no reason. Life is a cycle, behaviours carrying forward just as all life carries forward.

"So, my mother took his leadership away." Tagaaq took another long sip of water before ending the story. "Our laws would have said to send that man away, off to survive alone and live with his mistakes in solitude, but that is not what my mother wanted. He did not come into his place as a leader without reason. He had been a wise man and was respected in our community. To send him away would have been foolish and wasteful.

"My mother brought the man to the centre of the igluit, where all the camp had gathered. People told the man of his actions, told the whole village of his abuses. Out in the open, the man was shamed.

"Violence begets violence, Piturniq. The only way that the cycle is broken is by stopping that violence, by holding the abuser accountable, and by giving the victims the space and time to use their voices, to share their stories if they want to. Only if they want to.

"Once the victims shared their stories, the community held onto their voices. Together they all decided what to do, decided how to punish the abuser. They decided to give him one more chance. He no longer held a role in the village other than to be a provider, and he had to share all his future catches with everyone he had hurt to atone for the hurt he had caused.

"Do you know why I've told you this story?" Tagaaq asked.

Pitu shrugged at first. Their community was in the best condition it had ever been in. Everyone lived in mutual respect and mutual understanding. There were only one or two individuals Pitu could think of as problematic, but even they still provided for the betterment of their community.

He thought deeper about the story. *Perhaps it was a warning about what leadership could do to people,* Pitu thought. But that didn't make sense. What would be the point of having the story start off with Nagliktaujut Nunangat if that were the answer?

Pitu thought of the Naglitaujuit. He hadn't heard of them or of their place in the spirit world before. He pondered why this was important, why Tagaaq would care to tell this story at a time when they were all living well together and thriving. Were there things happening around him that he was unaware of?

Still, this did not seem to be the answer. Pitu shrugged once more as he thought even deeper. The Naglitaujuit lived in a cycle of being built up with reassurance and acceptance before spiralling back to their tormented state of mind. They never fully healed. As if they were brought back to their highest point of self-esteem, only to fall back to the lowest. They were incapable of living lives past their trauma.

"You told this story . . ." Pitu said, grasping at his thoughts, ". . . because true healing can only happen when we are alive and when the victims are given back their voices."

Tagaaq tilted his head and raised his shoulders in a half-shrug. "Yes, that is a part of it." Tagaaq yawned. "But I would ask you to ponder the story further. There is more to glean from it. Now, Piturniq, I think I must nap. Go, find your mother and your siblings. Make sure they know that you love them."

Pitu left the iglu. He didn't go straight to his mother, but instead made his way to check on his dogs. The team perked up at his arrival, lifting their heads from where they lazed about on the snow, wagging their tails in excitement. He brought a large piece of seal meat for them to share. Each dog ate their piece and fell asleep, except for Miki, his lead dog. Miki, with her one blue eye and one brown eye, sat straight, looking at Pitu with affection. He came to her and pet her fluffy fur coat. She nuzzled into him, sniffing fiercely at his caribou parka.

Last winter, Pitu had said to Miki that she was the only girl he needed. Now, as he kneeled next to the husky, thinking of Saima, he realized that he hadn't been truthful. There was no use in mourning something that he had never truly had, nor was there any use in mourning the change that was a natural part of life. He took a deep breath, said goodbye to Miki, and went to find his mother and his siblings.

3

Nightmares

Inside his iglu, the sounds of the village were muffled through the walls of snow. Pitu could barely hear the others. He was nestled under his blankets, trying to fall asleep but remaining restless. He tossed and turned, sat up, lay back down. As he lay there, wide awake and upset, he couldn't stop replaying what had happened hours ago in his head.

After eating with his family, Pitu had left his mother's iglu and began to make his way to his own. He'd built his iglu farther from the other igluit, away from the village. This was to ensure privacy as he spoke to Tiri or the other spirits who came to visit while he slept.

As he had been walking through the paths between the igluit, he saw Saima and Ijiraq entering her parents' iglu. For a moment, they didn't see Pitu. Ijiraq entered the iglu first, and just as Saima was about to crawl inside she looked over her shoulder and saw Pitu standing there.

"*Ainngai, angunasuktialuk*," she said, just loud enough for him to hear. "Hello, Great Hunter."

"*Saimaniq*," Pitu replied.

She looked away and entered the iglu without another word.

Saima was the only one who still called Pitu the Great Hunter. The rest of the village had begun to call him the *angakkuq*, the shaman.

It was almost laughable how quickly Pitu had forgotten his lesson with Tagaaq only hours before. His chest ached at the sound of Saima's voice. He sprinted to his iglu and called to Tiri to find a quick distraction, but even the spirits had nothing new to tell him.

Unable to stand the restlessness any longer, Pitu got dressed and left the iglu. He was hesitant to leave the village on his own now, afraid that the spirits would sweep him away on another dangerous journey. Instead, Pitu went to his *qamutiik* and took out a jig made from a caribou's antler, sinew, and a hook fashioned from the ivory of a walrus tusk. He made his way to a fishing hole in the ice kept open not too far from the village. There he was still able to see the huddled igluit, lit from within by the flames of the *qulliit*, the seal-oil lamps each iglu held.

He had never tried fishing in the middle of the night. Beneath the moonlight and the stars, all was silent and calm. The crisp air felt refreshing after the stuffiness of his iglu. He sat down on the ice next to the fishing hole, his right leg outstretched, his left folded in front of him. Pitu dropped the hook into the hole, let loose a long length of the sinew line, and began to jig the handle up and down slowly.

There were no bites for a long time. He sat, staring up at the beautiful moon. The northern lights—those vibrant streaks across the sky—were absent tonight. He thought of the time he had run with the lights in the other world, next to the spirit of his late father, and hundreds of other joyful spirits.

There was a slight tug on his line. Pitu began to pull it up quickly, but soon whatever he had caught was loose. *Probably a piece of seaweed,* he thought.

Again, a tug on the line. Stronger this time. He pulled, feeling that something was still caught in his hook. As he pulled the hook out of the water, he saw that he had

been right. A large chunk of tangled seaweed was caught in the hook. He untangled it and tossed it aside.

Pitu looked back to the fishing hole. He saw the water bobbing up and down as if a seal were coming up the hole to breathe. He almost dismissed it, thinking that it was still rippling caused by the seaweed.

He was about to toss the hook back in when he saw the face. He jumped, startled.

With disjointed speed, a qallupilluq with a familiar face of frightening beauty emerged from the hole, seaweed framing her features. As her shoulders came out of the hole, she reached her hands out toward him, her fingers elongated and tipped with claws. Pitu pulled himself backward with his arms, unable to look away as the creature crawled toward him.

"Piturniq," the qallupilluq said, her voice hoarse, but matching the face he cared for so deeply. "Piturniq, don't you love me? Won't you fight for me?"

Pitu stopped backing away, letting the qallupilluq with Saima's face reach him. Her claws dug into his legs, but he couldn't feel it. The creature smelled like the salt of the sea. As she crawled closer, she looked less and less like Saima. Her eyes became pure black, and her cheeks hollowed, her sharp teeth lengthening. He recognized this face, too. The qallupilluq he had killed.

"Nuliajuk knows what you did to me!" she shrieked viciously, deafening him. "She will punish you!"

Pitu finally pushed against her and found himself back in his iglu, half out of his bed. Sweat beaded down his chest, but he felt cold. The flame of his qulliq had been low, but now as he woke, it grew high enough to touch the curved wall of the iglu, and in the flame shadows danced. A feral face, beautiful and terrifying, stared at him for a moment before the flame withdrew back to its usual dimness.

He blinked against the light that obscured his vision. The stars and lines in his sight beat with the rhythm of his heart, and a lump grabbed hold of his throat as panic enveloped his whole body.

Tiri appeared and curled onto Pitu's lap. Her presence instantly brought him relief. Eventually, he calmed enough to lie back down, but he didn't fall back to sleep.

4

Mentor

Pitu waited outside his mother's iglu until she crawled out. She seemed to be in a rush, but when she noticed Pitu standing there staring at the moon, she asked him if he was okay.

He smiled tightly. "I am fine, *Anaana*."

From the look on her face, he knew that she didn't quite believe him. "You can go inside and wake Atiq. You and Natsivaq can take him hunting today."

Pitu listened to his mother. He went inside to wake his little brother. Atiq no longer slept the opposite way from everyone else on the bed, but he still slept spread-eagle, hogging the whole middle of the bed and giving Arnaapik only a sliver to herself. Pitu put his hand on Atiq's shoulder and shook him awake.

His little brother squinted. "*Eh-eh*," he whined. "Noooooo!"

"We need to get ready to go hunting, little brother," Pitu said. "So you can feed Anaana."

"You can feed her." Atiq pushed Pitu's hands away.

Trying to think of a way to wake him, Pitu remembered a story his father had told him about a demon who tickled his victims to death. Pitu started to wag his fingers as he said, "If you don't get up, Mahaha will come and tickle you until you laugh so hard you can't breathe!"

Atiq only mumbled in response. Pitu plunged his fingers into Atiq's ribs and began tickling him until he was laughing and kicking around the bed, struggling to get away. When he finally managed to free himself from Pitu's tickling fingers, he was wide awake. Atiq began to get dressed.

Pitu left and waited outside, resuming staring at the moon. It was full and bright, shining down on their little village. Pitu tried not to think of his dream, of how real it had felt. Looking at the moon helped him ignore it.

Atiq emerged from the iglu with a wide yawn. Pitu waited nearby as Atiq took a moment to stare at the horizon, a practice that ensured one a long life. The little brother then moved around to the back of the iglu and pulled down his caribou-skin pants to pee. Once he was finished, Atiq joined Pitu, and they made their way to Natsivaq's iglu.

Natsivaq was already outside, cutting up a large piece of caribou for breakfast. As Pitu and Atiq approached, Natsivaq cut off pieces of frozen meat and tossed them toward his two younger brothers. The three of them ate the caribou, interspersing each bite with brotherly banter. Natsivaq's treatment of Pitu had not changed since the discovery of his shamanic title, but Atiq was still uncomfortable with his older brother's spiritual power. Natsivaq began to tease the youngest of their family. "Oooh, Atiq, you better listen to Piturniq real good today, ai? If you displease him, he might send a spirit to eat you!"

Afraid that there was some truth to Natsivaq's words, Atiq began to tear up. He whined, "Take that back!"

As Atiq's lip trembled, Natsivaq snickered. Pitu held back his laughter, saying, "I wouldn't do that, little brother. The spirits would find you too bony."

Atiq immediately began to cry in response.

Natsivaq tapped the little boy's shoulders. "Yup, the age-old tradition of emotionally scarring the youngest child will never cease to bring me joy. Now, since we have honoured this tradition, our hunt will be successful. I'm sure of it."

Pitu laughed, remembering a trip ages ago when he was only four years old. On his first hunting trip with his father, Ujarasuk, Natsivaq had made similar jokes, saying that if he dawdled anytime during the hunt, they'd leave him to be eaten by polar bears.

Atiq continued to whimper as they loaded up the qamutiit and readied the dogs. He was still upset when they were ready to leave, so Pitu hugged his little brother tightly and whispered, "Little brother, the only thing I will ever ask of the spirits will be to protect you, even if you don't listen to me today."

The words eased Atiq and soon they headed out of the village.

Atiq ran alongside Pitu's dogsled, mimicking Pitu's speed and movements. Despite his reassurances that no spirits would come to haunt him, Atiq still listened carefully to all of Pitu's instructions. When Pitu asked Atiq to stop running and sit on the sled, he'd obey. When Pitu asked Atiq to keep watch for animal tracks, he would vigilantly look from side to side, searching for the presence of any animals.

They made sure to go farther out from their camp than usual, to give Atiq the privacy to learn his new skills. Typically, boys learned to hunt in large parties, and for the first few years, they were the brunt of much teasing between moments of praise for their developing skills. Atiq, however, was much too sensitive for these large hunting parties.

Since the loss of his biological parents, Atiq had faced many challenges. His grandmother, who had cared for him, had not been a particularly kind woman. After the loss of many children, she had grown careless in her words and wisdom. Atiq's birth had resulted in the loss of yet another child, and she had grown to resent the baby. For several years she had neglected him, leaving the baby, whom she refused to name, to be looked after by caring neighbours. Once Atiq's grandmother had passed away, Atiq had to learn to cope with the loss of his blood relatives.

The young boy knew that his grandmother had been bitter toward him and treated him with little love. He also knew that his new family was much kinder to him. However, his new family was aware that there was a part of him that would remember his grandmother and would wonder what his life would have been like if his parents had not died so young.

Pitu and Natsivaq teased Atiq playfully, but they never tried to hurt his feelings. They made sure that their teasing never had anything to do with his growth in learning, and they were always mindful to make sure he knew they were there for him. Even today, joking about the spirits, the two older brothers knew to reassure him that there was no truth to those words.

Soon, they would take Atiq on the large hunting parties, but they wanted to ensure that Atiq had basic skills first. He was much older than many other children learning to hunt, and this was due to the loss of Ujarasuk. As they grieved, the family had forgotten that Atiq was still a growing child in need of a mentor. The responsibility had fallen to Piturniq, but he had felt that he was too young to take on such a task. Now, Pitu felt ashamed of his selfishness.

Pitu began to show Atiq how to spot breathing holes in the ice. The mounds were imperceptible to the untrained eye, appearing simply as windswept snow atop the vast lengths of ice. Even up close, seeing that it was a breathing hole was difficult. Above the hole, the ice and snow made a dome, and at the very top of the dome was a tiny puncture, wide enough only to fit in a fingertip.

Atiq became good at spotting breathing holes instantly, and he'd point them out as they passed by the mounds. As the day became brighter, the sun creeping closer and closer to rising, they found more and more holes, until Pitu finally felt that one held promise.

The mound was tiny, smaller than the others. From it, he felt the gathering spirit of a seal slowly growing. "This one," he told Atiq. "You must stand facing the wind so it blows your scent away. You must plant your feet firmly, and even if your nose gets itchy, you cannot move. Do you understand, Atiq? Like this." Pitu stood facing the wind, planting his feet wide to remain balanced and comfortable. Atiq, holding onto his toy harpoon, copied his stance.

"You have to take your mitts off and hold your harpoon like this, little brother," Pitu continued, storing his mitts in his sleeves and holding the harpoon in his fingers, resting his arms on his thighs. The two brothers stood in line, hunched over the mound, clutching their harpoons. Pitu placed a piece of sinew on top of the breathing hole. "When the sinew blows away," he said, "that means a seal is there."

Since gaining his abilities, Pitu knew how to communicate with the animals of his land. As he stood there, the voice of the seal floated from beneath the ice. _For your little brother, Shaman, I will give myself to you._

The seal, however, did not come for breath right away. It waited until Pitu's fingers were freezing in pain. Atiq held firm, not fidgeting, not making a sound. After what felt like a lifetime, they could hear the water inside the mound begin to lap up and down.

As the seal emerged, the piece of sinew blew away and they could hear the seal's long, winded breaths inside. Excited, Atiq looked up at his brother. Pitu rose from his hunch, raising his arm and harpoon. After measuring time with three of his own deep breaths, Pitu used his strength to thrust the harpoon hard enough to break through the ice dome mound. He felt the tip strike the seal. Pitu firmly held on to the rope connected to the harpoon head and, without explanation, began to break the ice dome with his feet. Atiq quickly copied. Once he saw the seal, Atiq stumbled backward and made an excited, flabbergasted noise.

Pitu pulled the seal from the hole with ease. The seal snarled and growled but had little fight left in it. Pitu hit it over the head with his fist, and the seal's life faded. "Little brother, do you know what we do now?" he asked.

Atiq grabbed a handful of snow and tried to hand it to Pitu. "No, Atiq, this seal gave itself to you. You are the one who should give it a final drink of water."

The little boy, excited yet reverent, put the handful of snow into his mouth, using his own heat to melt it. Pitu knelt and opened the seal's mouth. Atiq followed suit, kneeling and putting his face next to the seal, his lips against the seal's mouth. He let the water run out in a steady stream. Smoothly the water went down the seal's throat, and its spirit drank. From within, Pitu could hear the seal's spirit. *Thank you, great shaman. Your little brother will be a great hunter one day.*

Pitu smiled, "Ai, Atiq. The seal thanks you."

Atiq echoed Pitu's smile, his eyes watery with joy and excitement. "Can we catch another one?"

5

Messenger

As the weeks carried on, Atiq swiftly learned how to become a hunter. He took his lessons very seriously and learned to hold his posture with strength. He ran with the dog team, helped Pitu steer the dogs, and untangled their harness lines.

The sun rose a little bit higher above the horizon every day, slowly melting the ice and snow of the land, bringing the bounty of spring. Each day, the people of the little village would rejoice in the sunlight and bask in its beautiful glow, which bathed the sky pink.

Pitu struggled through his lessons with Tagaaq. The elder was withering with age right before his eyes, and Pitu feared that soon the lessons would end. His fear grew as the sun rose, as Tagaaq's hair thinned and fell out. His wrinkles deepened with each of his stories. The spirits did not tell Pitu how to help Tagaaq. Instead, they told him that time was not as urgent as he thought. Tagaaq stumbled through his stories, and each one ended curtly, with little reflection on the meaning behind it.

Pitu's biggest fear was that the lessons would end before he learned all the ways of his power as a shaman, or the wisdom it took to be a good leader.

Teaching Atiq to hunt was the highlight of Pitu's days. Atiq grew into the habit of waking early and didn't need to be woken anymore. Instead he would emerge from the iglu as Pitu approached in the mornings. He quickly learned the proper method of butchering animals and how to stand without moving for hours. Within a couple of weeks, Atiq caught his first seal completely on his own.

As they were returning to camp after a hunt, manoeuvring around rough ice, Pitu caught sight of a soft blue light around the corner of an iceberg that stuck out from the vast frozen sea. He heard whispers floating with the wind.

He stopped the dog team to rest, and Natsivaq brought his team right next to his. The dogs of both teams mingled, and Natsivaq asked, "What is it?"

"Take Atiq back to camp with you," Pitu said. "I need privacy."

Natsivaq understood what he meant. Pitu ensured that his supplies were tied securely to his sled and flipped his qamutiik over to anchor the dogs. Atiq moved to Natsivaq's sled, but he hesitated. He looked at Pitu. "Don't go missing again, big brother."

Pitu nodded, the corners of his mouth turning up into a soft smile. "The spirits are nicer to me now."

Without another word, his brothers left. The wind called out to him again, no longer whispering, but urgent. He followed the voices to the blue light of the iceberg. Dozens of spirits called in unison. Pitu took off his mitts as he walked toward the iceberg, brushing his fingers against the fox-bone necklace he wore.

The voices on the wind grew louder and louder, booming by the time he reached the jagged piece of ice. One hand on his fox-bone necklace, Pitu placed his free hand onto the iceberg, closing his eyes.

Tiri appeared in his vision. He looked at the ethereal fox, her fur a shade of pure white to match the snow. Colourful tendrils of smoke wafted from her body, and in the smoke, Pitu could see the beautiful face of a woman, tattoos across her brow, cheekbones, and chin. Her hair was spread in many directions, as if floating in the wind.

Tiri spoke, *Nuliajuk calls to you.*

Pitu realized the woman he was seeing in the smoke was the Woman Below, a well-known sea spirit. All the animals from the ocean were Nuliajuk's children, and Pitu honoured her by respecting every animal he caught with a final drink of fresh water, or some other custom. Yet, he had also grown up fearing Nuliajuk. Any sign of disrespect and she could take the animals away, leaving the people above the sea to starve.

Pitu's heart hammered as he said, "I do not know how to answer her."

A camp to the south faces great strife, Tiri said, *Go to the camp. You will meet a shaman who will help you. Be careful of the company you keep. Nuliajuk will wait for you until the birth of seal pups.*

Pitu sped back to the village with his dog team, running alongside most of the way to make the trip go faster. As the village came into view, he saw that Atiq had waited at the edge of the igluit for his arrival. Pitu greeted his little brother and asked him to unpack the sled and feed the dogs. Atiq obliged, and Pitu went to the qaggiq.

The qaggiq was full of activity. Men played games of strength and endurance to woo the women. Young girls learned to throat sing and giggled every time one of them made a mistake. An elder told legends to children.

Tagaaq sat with his wife next to the storyteller. Pitu went to him, and Tagaaq looked at Pitu with one of his old smiles, full of humour and nonchalance.

"Piturniq!" Tagaaq greeted him. "How nice to see you, nephew."

Pitu hesitated, not wanting to tell Tagaaq what the spirits had told him. He was afraid he'd upset the old man and ruin the good mood. Tagaaq patted a seat on the bench made of hard-packed snow, urging Pitu to sit down. He did so, losing his urgency to share the news.

"Alaralak is telling the story of how narwhals came to live in our seas," Tagaaq murmured to Pitu.

The storyteller told the children of the young boy who had been a great hunter, who was blinded by his mother out of jealousy. A loon had helped the boy gain back his eyesight, but the son remained angry at his mother. The boy had asked for her help hunting a whale and tied the harpoon rope around her waist. The boy purposely threw his harpoon into a large beluga, and his mother was too weak to fight against the rope. She fell into the icy ocean and began to transform into a whale, her braid twisting into a tusk jutting from her head.

As a child, Pitu had quickly understood the meaning behind this story. Many people thought that the mother was the evil one in the story, and that the son had dealt her what she deserved. But Pitu never saw it that way. The mother did not represent evil, just as the son did not represent goodness. The story's meaning was much deeper—forgiveness and redemption. The son did not forgive his mother for the abuse she inflicted on him, leading him down a path to murder. In the end, the son could have chosen a different path, but it would not have ended with the creation of something beautiful. In a way, the mother had redeemed herself by becoming a narwhal, a creature of beauty and value.

Pitu sat there with the elders, listening to stories he'd heard since childhood. He forgot about what Tiri had told him, the urgent message leaving his mind. The stories the elder told reminded him of his journey to the spirit world.

Though he still had nightmares of the creatures he'd encountered and fought, Pitu couldn't help but feel a sense of greatness sweep into him. It wasn't the kind of vain greatness that made one radiate arrogance, but a greatness that made one in awe of the world. It was like standing at the edge of a glacier, hearing its voice as it cracked and moved, staring at a mass far too great to comprehend.

He had always known that his people believed in spirits, in beings and creatures of higher power and knowing. It was something that he had been taught since birth. It was something that could be seen in the way a woman could mimic the sounds of the environment through her chest and throat, the way a child had the same qualities of personality as their long-gone namesakes. Pitu had always known it, but experiencing the great magic of the world first-hand was something else entirely.

Time seemed to move slowly as he listened to the elder telling stories of Kiviuq, the greatest adventurer known to man. Kiviuq, who had travelled the world and found love in all places and people. People left the iglu and new people entered. He saw his mother come in with Arnaapik, his little sister, who now had tattoos lining her face as she matured into womanhood. Some time later, Atiq came in from playing outside, snot pouring from his nose to his lip in two lines. Pitu didn't know that hours had passed as he sat there listening.

Several stories later, Pitu saw a woman enter the qaggiq. She wore an amauti of distinct pattern, unique from their camp. She came in and stood in the centre of the dome, her eyes gazing intently into Pitu's. He was stunned by her beauty, her skin tanned as if she'd just been under the summer sun. Two braids framed her face, looped to the back of her head, and melted into the rest of her long brown hair. She was silent, but her eyes held power and surety.

Pitu stood up and walked toward her, forgetting that the qaggiq was full of other people who seemed not to see her. "*Kinauvit?*" he asked her. "Who are you?"

The woman kept her gaze strong, but she did not speak.

"Where did you come from?" Pitu asked.

Again, she did not answer.

The people in the qaggiq stopped their fun, turning to stare at Pitu in the centre of the iglu. He did not know if they could see her, too, but he continued. "Why have you come here?"

The woman opened her mouth and a great voice shook through the qaggiq. "*Nuliajuk has warned you, young shaman, and you disrespect her by not making haste. One more chance, and Nuliajuk won't be so forgiving next time.*"

A gust of wind blew snow into the qaggiq, and the woman faded, slowly turning into little snowflakes that the wind swept away.

6

Gathering

Those who had been inside the qaggiq when the spirit was there now gazed at Pitu with fright carved into their faces. The youth were confused, yet the adults clearly showed terror. The elders were silent, their faces unreadable.

Pitu found himself surrounded by hostility. Never had a spirit entered a qaggiq in any of their camps, and he wondered if the villagers thought of this incident as a failure of his shamanic powers, or as only the beginning of a lifetime of spirits invading their sacred space of celebration.

He didn't know how to calm everyone down. With each passing second, he could feel the tension rising.

"This afternoon," Pitu said, brushing his fingers on his necklace, "my tuurngaq told me of Nuvuk, a camp to the south that is facing hardship. I must leave tomorrow so that I can help them."

There was a murmur. Pitu's mother stood and went to him in the middle of the iglu. He could see tears glistening in her eyes, but her voice was strong as she addressed the qaggiq. "Our shaman has been summoned by Nuliajuk herself," she said. "And we mustn't be afraid of what may happen. However, I am still his mother, and my heart is still healing from when the spirits took him from me this winter. Piturniq must leave. There is no arguing on that, but a hunting party must accompany him and keep him safe for me."

"Yes, I agree with Inuuja," Tagaaq said, amusement playing into his voice. "Piturniq is known among the spirits for his great power, and for his goodness. Everyone wants a piece of him!"

The tension began to thin with Tagaaq's joke. He continued, "We are lucky to have him with us, and we shouldn't let him slip away so easily. Three hunters should accompany him on his journey."

Atiq stood up first, his boyish face dirty with a mixture of snot and food. "*Uvanga!* I'll go!"

The people in the qaggiq laughed. Pitu smiled, "I would be honoured to have my little brother come."

"Atiq can go," Inuuja said, her lips a thin line. "But he is only a child. We still need three hunters to go along with Piturniq."

Sitting beside Saima, Ijiraq said, "I will accompany Piturniq on his journey."

Pitu felt dread leaking into his stomach. The two young men had interacted very little, and truthfully, Pitu didn't feel any animosity from Ijiraq himself. A part of Pitu's reaction stemmed simply from jealousy. Ijiraq was respectful and incredibly helpful, but he was still Saima's husband. Pitu tried to put his dread aside. He welcomed Ijiraq with a slight lift of his chin, and the hunter mirrored the movement back to him.

Tagaaq's son and Pitu's cousin, Qajaarjuaq, volunteered next, and Pitu was soon filled with a deeper sense of dread mixed with anxiety. Since last fall, Qajaarjuaq had outwardly shown his dislike of Pitu's role as a leader, and even more so now as a shaman. Pitu repeated the gesture of lifting his chin in welcome to the man, but he felt no kinship toward him.

The last volunteer was a hunter named Tumma, a boy born the summer before Pitu. They had grown up as friends, and Pitu felt a small hint of relief that there would at least be one friend on this journey.

Pitu nodded at the three hunters. "Rest well tonight. We will leave tomorrow."

Pitu woke to strands of long hair tickling his face. He opened his eyes and saw her brown eyes, her black hair falling down. She smiled sheepishly at him. He thought it was another dream, but he could smell her and feel her breath.

"Saimaniq?" he whispered. "What are you doing here?"

"Piturniq the Loud Sleeper," she whispered back. "Your snoring can be heard all over the camp."

He laughed as he felt the blood rushing to his cheeks. He had been asleep, so he was slow to react to her presence, sitting over him in his iglu. Just on the other side of the caribou-skin blankets, he was naked, except for the necklace he never took off. He stayed still, hoping that she couldn't see his blushing in the dim light. He made himself say, "You shouldn't be here."

Saima leaned away from him then, wrapping her arms around her knees. Pitu sat up slightly, resting his weight on his elbows. The mischief had left her, and he could see her vulnerability. She murmured, "I had to see you before you left again."

A rush of emotion swept through Pitu. She was afraid that he would go missing again, just as his family was. He knew that they were breaking rules right now, that the people of the camp wouldn't approve of this late-night visit, but he still gestured her to come closer to him. He sat up, making sure that the caribou blanket covered his private parts. Saima crawled over and sat with her legs under her, facing him. She put her hand in his.

"I know I'm not supposed to be here, Piturniq," she said. "Just because you are a shaman doesn't mean you're the wisest person here."

"I never said I was the wisest person here," Pitu said. "But a wise person wouldn't risk angering the spirits as this visit might."

"The spirits have always liked me," she laughed lightly. "It'll take more than a visit to a friend's iglu to make them angry at me."

She spoke with such certainty, such lightness, her voice so free of care. He replied, "Perhaps, but I fear that the spirits are not as fond of me."

She squinted her eyes in the darkness. She reached up and traced the lines of his scars from the qallupilluit, most of which had faded. He felt heat follow the path of her fingertips but said nothing. Saima smiled again, softly. "I fear that may be true, but what would our lives become if we chose to always please the spirits? What is life if we do not take risks?"

"When did you become so rebellious?"

Her smile grew then. He could see her teeth behind her lips. "I have been this way since I was born, you silly boy."

They bantered on for quite some time. Saima always teased him and spoke with an air of higher knowing, as if she were the one who could hear what the wind was saying and he was just another dumb boy. He enjoyed listening to her amused whispers and her quick, witty responses to whatever he said.

They spoke for hours, catching up as old friends do who hadn't seen each other for years. She asked, "How do you sleep so soundly when you are alone? I've always had trouble sleeping without my family around."

"Well, Atiq used to kick me in his sleep, so it's nice to have the space." He curled his mouth into a smile. "But usually I consult with spirits in my sleep."

"Tell me of these spirits." She yawned. "Are you always busy with your work?"

"I dream," he explained. "But in those dreams, I am speaking with ghosts and creatures of the other worlds."

She asked him questions about his journey, about the spirits he heard and saw each night, and whether the stories he told at Qaggiq were true. He answered everything honestly, telling her that he altered some details about each event when he told his stories at celebration. He didn't tell her about some things, such as the children he found in the amauti of the qallupilluq, or the tricks that the polar bear pets did for Inukpak. Somehow, he felt that those were things only meant for him.

"Sometimes," she whispered, her tone becoming melancholy and serious, "I wish that I had run away after you went missing. I wish that I'd gotten lost and only you would have been able to find me. If I'd done that, I would not have to be with Ijiraq. I'd be free to choose my own fate. Imagine that? But I can't. And Ijiraq is too good a man to . . . ."

Pitu squeezed her hand. He could see it all, the life they would have had if things had been different. If he hadn't gotten lost in the blizzard, if he hadn't gone to the land of spirits. Then they would be together, exactly as they were now, only they wouldn't need to sneak around at night. Pitu wouldn't have the feeling of guilt clawing inside his chest. Pitu wanted to ask, *Is Ijiraq that good of a man? Does he deserve you? What is stopping us from breaking the arrangement?*

As quickly as the jealousy boiled up, it simmered away. Saima knew herself better than Pitu knew himself. She was more in control of her own fate than she let on, and they both knew that.

Instead of thinking of what could have been, he decided instead to be there with her in that very moment. They talked some more, never touching more than their holding hands. They laughed carelessly, like they had when they were children.

At the end, she placed a *kunik*, a kiss of breath, on his cheek. Pitu leaned away, surprised by it. She chuckled. "For a man of your fortitude, you embarrass so easily."

Pitu just laughed, not knowing what to say.

"Goodbye, Piturniq the Great Hunter," she said as she crawled off the bedding and stood. She made her way to the ice porch of his iglu. She looked back, saying, "I hope I will see you again."

He said the same to her, and she left him there alone. He lay back in bed, feeling a sense of closure, some sense of finality.

There was a part of him, though, a tiny, mischievous part of him, that held onto the moment. That small part of him placed it deep in his mind. A moment to remember when he was lonely or sad. A reminder of a small bit of love that was different from his family's love, and that was much more than friendship. He held it so deeply inside of him, he hoped it hadn't just been a dream.

7

Journey

Though he felt rested and well, Pitu emerged from his iglu to a thick grimness among the people of camp. Ijiraq and Tumma were already preparing their supplies for the trip, their eyelashes and wispy beards becoming frosty in the morning air. Others of the village watched the men prepare. Pitu joined the two hunters to pack the qamutiit and prep the dogs for their long run.

He was sure that some people knew of Saima's midnight visit, particularly Ijiraq, but the man said nothing. Pitu felt a small sense of guilt as he greeted Ijiraq good morning, and the man replied with a casual smile.

Atiq ran from his mother's iglu, shrieking, "DON'T FORGET ME!"

"Ai, Atiq," Pitu said. "We're not going to leave you."

"Oh," Atiq said, out of breath. They chuckled at Atiq's moment of hysterics. The little boy was embarrassed by the laughter at first, but he soon joined in. Pitu looked around at the villagers watching them, not seeing the face he was looking for.

"Where is Qajaarjuaq?" Pitu asked.

"He's taking his time," Tumma answered. "He said, 'This is the great shaman's calling; he should do the hard work.'"

"Argh," Ijiraq grunted. "Why did he volunteer to join us if he's going to act like a child?"

Pitu turned to look at Ijiraq, seeing his own annoyance mirrored on the other man's face. Pitu felt a sudden sense of brotherhood as he murmured quietly so the onlookers wouldn't hear, "You don't like him, either?"

"Does anyone?" Ijiraq retorted. The three hunters laughed.

They finished packing up their supplies. They'd take three dog sleds for this journey to Nuvuk; Pitu and Atiq would take one, Ijiraq and Tumma would take another, and Qajaarjuaq would have his own. They tied all their supplies tightly to the qamutiit and ate some frozen caribou. Soon, their tasks were all complete, and Qajaarjuaq was still nowhere in sight.

Families came forward to say their goodbyes. Pitu kissed his mother on the cheek, reassuring her that he would return safely and that he would not go missing again. She handed him something bundled tightly in sealskin. "It's _pissi_," she said, "dried fish. For when your travelling partners are in low spirits. Bribe them with it to ensure they bring you back to me."

Pitu looked at the bundle with a tinge of disbelief. "How did you save this since last summer?" he asked.

"My son, you are a shaman," she murmured, "but you don't know everything. A mother shouldn't reveal her secrets. Now go, say goodbye to your sister."

He hugged Arnaapik tightly. He said to her, "Wait until I'm back before you get yourself married. Ai, little sister?"

Arnaapik blushed and stuck out her tongue. "Yuck, I don't need a husband. I'm not going to get married before you."

"You're probably going to be single your whole life then," Pitu laughed, glad to hear her view of marriage. He looked over his shoulder to see Tumma. Growing up, Tumma had always been especially kind to Arnaapik. Pitu had always thought that the two liked each other. He looked back at Arnaapik and said, "Perhaps your future husband is coming with me on my journey."

She looked over Pitu's shoulder at Tumma and raised an eyebrow in confusion. "Tumma?" she laughed. "No way."

He laughed. But he had seen her cheeks go bright red, from something other than the cold. Arnaapik moved on from Pitu and went to say her goodbyes to Atiq. Pitu eavesdropped as she hugged their little brother and quietly said, "You take care of him, okay? Don't lose him."

"*Iilaak*," Atiq raised his eyebrows in agreement. "I know."

Pitu felt a small pang in his chest, a vein bursting with affection. He walked away, patted his lead dog, Miki, on the muzzle, and watched the hunters finish up their goodbyes. Tumma hugged his grandmother and his parents. Atiq hugged Anaana, and Ijiraq hugged Saima.

Tagaaq came up to Pitu, a hand outstretched to shake. "I must warn you, the spirits are anxious," he said. "Don't trust my son, Piturniq. He does not mean well on this journey."

Pitu agreed by raising his eyebrows, grasping Tagaaq's hand in a strong hold. "I feel apprehensive about him, too."

"Leave now," Tagaaq said, a slight smile lighting up his face. "Perhaps with a head start, Qajaarjuaq will be too lazy to go to the trouble of catching up."

Pitu let go of Tagaaq's hand, replying, "I will miss our lessons, Uncle."

"*Uvangattauq*." The elder agreed. "Me too."

And with that, the hunters and their dog teams took off across the tundra toward the ocean that was frozen with ice thick by twice their height. Behind them, the village of igluit grew smaller, and with it, their loved ones.

The route they travelled was smooth. The dogs ran swiftly, often getting their lines tangled. The hunters took many short breaks to fix the harnesses and eat a bit of meat before continuing their trek.

The horizon was covered in the orange glow of the sun, the clouds in the sky painted pink. The ice and snow gleamed, crystals shining in the air and upon the ground. The hunters felt lucky for the *silattiaq*, the beautiful weather. On days like this Pitu sometimes forgot about the cold, the brutal blizzards, and the shivering that gripped him on bad days. *Sila*, the environment, the air, and the world around them, often found ways to make one feel fortunate. When Sila was in good spirits, the people were happy. When Sila was unhappy, it often meant that there were problems within the community. It was an indicator that someone in a village was being untruthful or immoral, leading bad spirits to bring suffering in any way they chose.

The group basked in the glow of the day. Though they travelled long and far, they went at a leisurely pace. Pitu was surprised at how well the hunters were working together. He had known Tumma all his life and they had always been good friends, but neither of them knew Ijiraq very well. It turned out that Ijiraq had many of the same qualities they had.

It was easy to forget that Ijiraq was married to Saima. Pitu got along with him so well that they were soon making each other laugh without effort. Even Atiq was in a good mood. Atiq was shy, and he wasn't the sharpest harpoon on the qamutiik. It took him a while to understand the jokes that were being told, but he remained upbeat and positive.

The sun had long set by the time they stopped to sleep. They built their igluit by the moonlight. Atiq was eager to learn how to cut blocks, so Pitu let him try a couple. Once the domed snow houses were up, the men were tired from a good day of travelling. They made sure the dogs were all fed, and then they went inside for the night.

Atiq and Pitu shared their iglu, while Tumma and Ijiraq slept in the other. Pitu's dread over Ijiraq's presence and Qajaarjuaq's impending arrival had left him after a day full of easy-going attitudes. Pitu hoped that Qajaarjuaq decided not to catch up.

That night, Pitu spoke with Tiri. They met within the iglu while Atiq snored next to Pitu. She snuck around the bedding, curling up close to him. "The journey has begun well," he said.

Yes, I am glad of that, she replied. *But your hopes of Qajaarjuaq staying behind are not good thoughts to have. He will come, and you must be accepting of the consequences his presence will have. Do you not remember my warning? Be careful of the company you keep.*

"I remember, but there was little I could do other than accept. Denying him in front of the whole community would have brought more trouble," Pitu said. He couldn't understand how a man could live in such a negative state of mind. Qajaarjuaq found a reason to complain about everything, and he especially found reasons to complain about Pitu. Somehow, Qajaarjuaq knew the exact words to say that ate at one's soul, as if he could sniff out insecurities and bring them to life out in the open. "I don't have any good feelings toward him."

He brings trouble that you must learn to deal with, my dearest.

"Tell me about the village we are going to," Pitu said, eager to change the topic.

*They are starving. I fear that their struggles
have not yet all come to light.*

"What do you mean?"

*A strangeness hangs in the air there. The people
are hiding something.* Tiri licked Pitu's arm. *You will
face much more than a meeting with Nuliajuk. The
spirits there are old, festering things. They need you.*

With that, Pitu decided the conversation could
rest. He would understand Tiri's warnings soon
enough, and he didn't like the thought of ancient spirits
awaiting him. He was frightened.

The fright bled into the rest of his dreams. He
saw the black wolves as he slept. They didn't attack
him, only silently stalked him as he walked across the
tundra. In the darkness, they stared, their yellow eyes
reflecting against the snow.

8

Origin

Out of restlessness and nightmares, Pitu decided it was time to get up. Ijiraq was already outside preparing their supplies when Pitu emerged from the iglu. They nodded at one another in a friendly way. The two had become friends on their journey and had quite easily grown used to each other.

The fatigue must have shown on Pitu's body. Ijiraq began the conversation. "*Qanuinnavit?* What's wrong?"

"Just a dream," Pitu answered, neglecting to mention that it involved his tuurngaq and evil spirits. A nightmare on the first night of a journey would definitely raise tension among the hunters.

"Mmm," Ijiraq mumbled, deep in thought. An awkward silence developed between them. Though they got along well, there were still some things about Ijiraq that bothered Pitu. The fact that he was Saima's husband wasn't the only reason he felt uneasy around him. His name was the name of a type of shapeshifter, creatures that can take many forms and are difficult to detect. The creature's only weakness was its red eyes, which it could hide for only short periods of time. Though Ijiraq didn't have red eyes, Pitu had difficulty feeling at ease with the name. His whole life, Pitu had been told that names had deep meaning and connection to spirit. He wondered why Ijiraq's parents had named him after a creature of wicked nature.

Just as Pitu was going to walk away, Ijiraq spoke again. "I knew that she was betrothed to you, Piturniq."

Pitu looked back at Ijiraq, unsure of what to say.

"The first time I asked to marry her, Saima's parents, Amarualik and Panninguaq, told me about you," Ijiraq continued. "I respected your arrangement. Then you disappeared. The whole village was mourning your loss, and it seemed the animals had also disappeared. We struggled for the first few weeks of your disappearance, and I saw Saima's family was not doing well. I asked again, and her parents agreed for the sake of hunger, knowing that it would be easier to provide for their family this way."

Pitu looked down at the dogs. He'd been told of the animals leaving when he was swept away by the blizzard. Tagaaq had said that the animals were attracted to the aura that Pitu gave off. When he disappeared, the animals searched for his scent, but could not find him.

"Saima hated me at first," Ijiraq said. "She refused to stay with me. She told me that you would come back. She would leave our iglu at night and spend most nights with your dog team."

Pitu looked toward his own dogs, sleeping in the moonlight.

"After a couple of weeks, she started to warm up to me. We spent more time together on our own, and we became friends more than husband and wife. I understood that she was grieving. Eventually, our relationship went further . . . until the day you returned."

He remembered coming back and being found by the hunters. His return to camp was joyful and hopeful. Until Pitu had gone to see his dogs for the first time in weeks. Saima had snuck over to see him and had told him about her marriage to Ijiraq. Pitu waited for Ijiraq to continue.

"I know I am the one who is keeping you both apart. I know it," Ijiraq said. "But I can't bring myself to leave, to let you two be together. I love her, and I think she was growing to love me in return. I have been nothing but kind to her and her family."

Pitu spoke, his voice shaking as it broke past a lump in his throat. "She deserves a man like you."

Ijiraq furrowed his brow. "Everyone looks at me like I have taken her away from you."

Pitu shook his whole body in discomfort, knowing that he had played a part in that. All his longing stares were not hidden from the eyes of others. Pitu didn't know what to say. He hadn't been expecting this conversation to happen so early in their journey.

A certain amount of respect built up within Pitu, and he found himself staring at Ijiraq. Most times, Pitu found himself shaking his head at other people, thinking that wisdom shouldn't be so hard to find. Though their livelihood was constantly on a precipice, hanging by the thread of catching food to eat or on the whims of the weather, people were often very self-involved. They thought most often of themselves rather than the betterment of the camp.

Now, Ijiraq stood before him, a man only slightly older than he, and wisdom came off him in waves. Pitu heard the good spirits as they swarmed toward them, attracted to their relaxed temperament. They whispered of good tidings.

For months, Pitu had been aching for Saima, feeling sorry for himself and what they could have been. But now he closed off a part of himself from her. His conversation with her the night before had helped him to overcome some of the pain he felt.

He thought of how stressful being the wife of a shaman could be, how much it might change what he loved about Saima. She was joyful and clever. Every time he'd leave camp to go hunting, she'd worry that he would never return. He thought of the shaman who had trained him, Taktuq, and then he thought of what had happened to Taktuq's family.

"I can admit that I am still upset that you came along, but I am learning to live with it." Pitu thought harder. Lightheartedly, he joked, "Besides, Saima isn't the kind of person who simply follows what people tell her to do. She must care for you if she hasn't come running to me . . . yet."

Ijiraq offered a tight-lipped smile. Pitu could see he was uncomfortable. Ijiraq said, "I have no idea what she plans to do, but I don't want you to interfere anymore. Try to let her go."

Pitu hung his head slightly. "Yes," he said. "I'll do my best."

Another silence fell upon them. Not quite comfortable, but not quite awkward either. For a moment, they simply stood in the blowing wind.

Finally, Pitu asked, "Why did your family name you Ijiraq?"

The other man sighed, as if he had been anticipating this question. With his shaman's eye, Pitu could see spiritual blue smoke lifting from Ijiraq's shoulders. Ijiraq replied, "My mother had a dream where I was saved by an ijiraq when she was pregnant with me."

"Oh?" Pitu said. "Do you know this dream?"

Ijiraq raised his eyebrows to affirm that he did know the dream, and the two sat down upon their sleds. The sky slowly brightened as Ijiraq began to tell the story.

"Before I was born, my parents and siblings were travelling to visit my mother's family in another camp. They stopped for a day in a beautiful spot, and my mother fell asleep while my father and my older brother set up camp and my sisters played. My mother was very tired from the journey, so they all left her sleeping. She dreamt of a little boy following lemmings from their burrows underneath the rocks.

"While my mother slept, my father's dog team began to howl. There was a polar bear approaching camp. My father prepared to protect everyone.

He grabbed his harpoon and strode toward the approaching bear. My mother heard the dogs in her dream. She had also dreamed of a polar bear coming toward camp, but there were two polar bears: a young cub and a mother. She dreamt of the little boy running past a large boulder. The mother bear emerged from the other side of the boulder and attacked him."

He continued, "My mother screamed and ran toward the bear, but she was too far away to stop the attack, her dream making her running steps seem slow and lethargic. Then, the lemming the boy had been following came out from its burrow, its eyes a bright shade of red. It looked at the polar bear and . . . transformed. It copied the bear's shape, and suddenly they began to fight. My mother watched the shapeshifter fight the bear. My mother decided to name me Ijiraq so that the shapeshifter would recognize me if her dream came true."

A short silence followed while Pitu thought about this. He considered the value of a mother knowing her child's true name, even if the name honoured a creature known to be terrifying and violent. He asked, "So, did her dream come true?"

"No," Ijiraq laughed. He was quiet for a second, then he added, "Not yet, anyway."

They continued talking, exchanging tales from their lives. Pitu told Ijiraq about how he had returned from the spirit world, about the sacrifice his friend had made. They changed the topic from their harrowing journeys to the jokes of life and more joyful things.

In the distance, they could hear the cries and huffing of an approaching dog team. Across the vast sea ice, they could see the lone dog team and its hunter. Somehow, they both knew that it was Qajaarjuaq.

Tumma emerged from his iglu, groggy-eyed and lazy. He took a couple of strides to pee, then came to stand next to where Pitu and Ijiraq sat. Pitu's oldest friend mumbled, "So, he decided to show up after all."

A heaviness grew among the three as Qajaarjuaq came closer and closer.

Even Atiq came out of the iglu to see the last hunter's approach. He went to Pitu's side, tense and silent.

Before his dog team had even stopped moving, Qajaarjuaq was barking at the group. "You think you can get rid of me? I'm a part of this group, too, don't forget!"

He jumped from his qamutiik and came up to them. Pitu stood. Qajaarjuaq came close, standing nose-to-nose with Pitu in an act of intimidation. The older man fumed, while Pitu remained calm. Tiri's voice whispered to him to stay composed in his mind. If she hadn't been there to calm him, Pitu was sure that he would have become just as angry as Qajaarjuaq. He took a step back.

"You think that was funny? Huh?" Qajaarjuaq snarled.

"No," Pitu said. "But I have to remind you that the spirits told us to rush."

Qajaarjuaq growled but said nothing. The calm of the group seemed to make him think twice. He narrowed his eyes and looked at the others.

Pitu gestured to his iglu. "Qajaarjuaq, you can take my iglu. We will let you rest for a couple of hours before we have to head out again."

The tension was still thick as Qajaarjuaq accepted the terms. Perhaps he was too tired to argue, for after only a short moment of breath after crawling into the iglu, Qajaarjuaq's snoring enveloped the camp.

The hunters made their preparations. Ijiraq and Tumma went to catch a seal or two before the next leg of their journey.

"Big brother," Atiq whispered. Pitu looked at his little brother while they were cutting caribou meat to feed Qajaarjuaq's dogs. He turned his chin upward to show that he was listening. "Qajaarjuaq scares me."

Pitu reached out a hand and patted Atiq's shoulder. Trying to be reassuring, Pitu said, "He's going to be a challenge."

"No." Atiq shook himself out of Pitu's grip and faced him. "He's going to do something. I just know it. He's going to do something bad to you."

Pitu could see how upset Atiq was. "How do you know?" he asked.

Atiq looked down and put a piece of the frozen caribou into his mouth. He chewed for a good long moment before he answered. "Natsivaq told me."

Pitu hugged his little brother for a moment. "We're all uncomfortable about what he is doing on this journey, but Qajaarjuaq will provide good lessons to learn from, okay? We have to remember to treat him with respect, even if he will not treat us that way."

They bickered back and forth until the other hunters came back with a seal. Ijiraq strapped the seal to the qamutiik, and the four of them ate pieces of caribou while they waited for Qajaarjuaq to stop snoring.

9

Nuvuk

Once Qajaarjuaq graced the others with his presence and tirelessly foul mood, they continued their journey. Though Qajaarjuaq was the oldest of the hunters, he complained without end. Whether it was about how they had left without him the day before, or that he was starving, or that he was running his dog team without assistance, he found a way to make the rest of them feel like it had been their fault his life was so terrible.

Tumma, tired of the complaining, decided to run with Qajaarjuaq's team. Ijiraq was fine with running his dog team alone, and they all hoped that the help would calm Qajaarjuaq down.

It didn't work. Qajaarjuaq effortlessly found more things to complain about each day of their trip. He would scold Tumma for running too slow or for veering the dogs off course. He'd tell the others they were running too fast and the dogs would tire too soon. He'd say they were taking too many breaks to let the dogs rest. He'd tell them they had to eat more; then at the next stop he'd say they were eating too much.

Each passing day of the journey, Pitu grew more exhausted—not from the physical exertion, but from the frustration of small abuses from Qajaarjuaq. By the time their three igluit were built at the end of each day, the four younger hunters were drooping from fatigue, only a moment away from collapsing on the caribou- and polar bear–skin beds inside.

"Tah," Qajaarjuaq would scoff, "you guys are younger than me and you're more tired than I am? Kids these days are so lazy."

The beautiful weather that had been with them since the beginning of their trip slowly faded with each day. One day, they emerged from their igluit to find an overcast sky, with the approach of a whiteout blizzard. The hunters secured their supplies, putting valuable objects into their dwellings. They built half-domed shelters to protect the dogs from the approaching storm.

Pitu tried not to think of what the approaching storm reminded him of. He would not be swept away by the blizzard as he had been before. He knew his purpose now.

The storm raged on for days, leaving the travellers to huddle in their igluit in boredom. They had all gathered into Pitu's iglu and were eating boiled meat to warm themselves while the wind blew outside. Atiq, the most bored of them all, complained and whined without mercy.

"Come on, big brother, come *onnnn*!" he whined. "I just want to play outside or something. It's okay when I play out in blizzards back home!"

"You can't play outside!" Pitu snapped. It was their third day cooped up inside, and Pitu was tired of his little brother. It seemed that Atiq had learned well from Qajaarjuaq. "Back home there are more people to look after you, there's more cover, and you know the land better. You remember what happened to me the last time I was caught in a blizzard?"

Atiq stopped complaining, instead trying to find games to play inside. He tied a length of sinew together into a circle and started to play string games. Once he'd grown tired of this, he started to play with seal bones as if they were dolls. Once he'd grown tired of this, he started to play string games again. This cycle continued.

"I'm *soooo booooored*!" Atiq whined.

"Shh!" Pitu snapped back.

Tumma laughed. "Come on, Piturniq. You want me to take him outside for a bit? I'm feeling restless too."

Hesitantly, Pitu agreed. Tumma and Atiq put their over-parkas on, rushing to get outside. Tumma started out with Atiq close on his tail. At the last second, Atiq looked back at Pitu and said, "Don't worry, big brother. If we get lost in the storm, the spirits will help you find us, right?"

"Don't say another word, little brother," Pitu said through his clenched jaw, "or I'll change my mind."

Atiq laughed and ran away. Pitu could still hear their voices when they were outside, which lessened his worry. Pitu, Ijiraq, and Qajaarjuaq remained quiet inside, awkward but not tense. It seemed that even boredom quieted a well-known complainer such as Qajaarjuaq.

The next morning, the storm had passed. The journey continued.

With the continuation of their trip came the resurgence of Qajaarjuaq's terribly annoying voice. Soon, his previous complaints and reprimands returned, and the group settled into the familiar routine of ignoring him again.

One night, Pitu waited until the other three had entered their igluit. Qajaarjuaq was about to enter his own, but Pitu said, "Is there something wrong, Qajaarjuaq?"

In the wind, Pitu could hear the spirits asking him to take caution. He listened to their warnings with great care.

Qajaarjuaq stopped and turned to look at him. "There are many things wrong, *Angakkuq.*" He spat the last word, Pitu's title as a shaman, as an insult. He didn't elaborate.

"I fear that leaving those things unspoken will create great hardship on our journey," Pitu said after a moment of silence, remaining calm. He tried to sound encouraging, holding the anger that encroached upon him at a distance. Just out of reach, but not far enough that Pitu could forget it was there. "Actually, I think it already has. Tell me what is troubling you."

Qajaarjuaq chuckled. His laugh did not echo his father's laid-back humour. Instead, it was a show of haughtiness to infer that he knew more than Pitu did, that Pitu's qualms and worries were unfounded and unneeded. Though Pitu knew not to fall for it, he couldn't stop that feeling of inferiority from springing up within.

It enraged Pitu to feel this judgment from a man who treated those around him with such little esteem. Still, the voices in the wind urged Pitu to keep calm.

"I have no troubles to share with _you_, Angakkuq," Qajaarjuaq said through his chuckling. "You've fooled our people, but I know that you are weak. You are scared."

"The sooner we talk about this," Pitu said, balling his hands into fists, "the sooner we will resolve our differences. You have to remember that we are taking this trip to help people who are suffering. We can't bring our own problems with us. And I admit that I am scared. I am not embarrassed by that."

Qajaarjuaq turned away, ignoring Pitu. He kneeled in the snow, ready to crawl into the iglu. Briefly, he looked again at Pitu. He said, "I don't tell my troubles to children." With that, he entered his iglu, leaving Pitu alone in the cold.

Pitu went inside his iglu. Atiq had already managed to fall asleep, his limbs spreading out and taking up most of the open space on the furs.

Pitu's blood was still rushing with anger. He sat at the foot of the bed, hunched over to rest his elbows on his knees. It took several deep breaths before he started to feel the rush of adrenaline and fury fade. Once he could focus on the fading feeling, the resentment ebbed away, leaving only exhaustion.

He undressed, got under the blankets, and fell asleep. For once, his dreams had nothing to do with spirits. He dreamt of a warm summer day, basking in the sunlight in his *qajaq*, floating in the water. It felt as though he was drinking the light in, storing it in his whole being, his whole spirit.

In the waters surrounding him, whales surfaced, accompanied by seals and fish. Each whale sprayed breath from its blowhole. Instead of the odour of whale breath, however, Pitu could smell the scent of sorrel and blueberries from the hillsides.

He woke feeling well rested and serene.

He was first to emerge from the igluit. He went to his dog team, checking for injuries from midnight fights and making sure they were not hungry. For the most part, the dogs treated Pitu just as a hunting partner, another relationship that was integral to survival in their treacherous environment. Only Miki treated Pitu with affection, often jumping up to his chest to lick his face.

He tightened the ropes holding the qamutiik together and made sure the hunting gear was strapped down just as tightly. Then he sat on the sled, and he waited.

The day grew brighter, but it was cloudy and overcast. Pitu took his *iggaak*, sunglasses made from caribou antler, from a sealskin pouch strapped to the sled and tied them onto his head. It didn't take long for the rest of the group to wake and come outside. None of them reflected the peace that was within Pitu. He didn't let that bother him.

Without a word, each hunter ate his morning meal. Pitu watched as Atiq struggled to cut meat for himself, until finally Atiq looked at his older brother and sheepishly asked for help. Pitu took out a sealskin-wrapped bundle. He tossed it to his little brother and said that there was enough for the rest of the hunters to share. Atiq opened it to find the dried fish his mother had given to Pitu before they left home.

Qajaarjuaq refused the gesture, insisting that he did not like the taste of fish at the end of winter.

It was of no concern to Pitu, and the fish seemed to have the desired effect on the others. Their mood lifted as they ate the fish. By this time of year, the dried fish is usually long gone, having been devoured by the end of fall, but somehow Anaana had managed to save some for this precise moment. Pitu had hoped to save it for much later in the journey, for a bad day.

Today was not a bad day, but the previous days definitely had been.

Soon, only one good piece of the dried fish was left. Again, Pitu offered it to Qajaarjuaq as a peace offering.

"Fine," he said as he grabbed it.

Though Qajaarjuaq didn't betray his usual hostility, Pitu saw a flicker of mirth when he bit off a piece of the fish. Frozen fish was good, but dried fish was something else entirely. In the summer, the fish were cut in half lengthwise, still connected by the tail. The filets were cut into cubes attached by the skin, then the fish were hung upside down on racks made from animal bones stacked upon boulders and mounds of rocks. The fish dried for days, with the sun beating down on it twenty-four hours a day. During the winter, a summer treat such as this was rare, refreshing, and good for morale.

The gesture had helped. Their journey that day was smooth. Not perfect, but the tension was alleviated. Qajaarjuaq did not find as many things to complain about as he had before. The others were quiet, but their good humour slowly returned. The ease lingered for the next few days as they continued onward.

The other hunters learned to ignore Qajaarjuaq and his complaints and demands. They never came to the point of becoming friends with him, or even being on good terms with him, but Qajaarjuaq didn't seem to mind. He began joking around more instead of whining. But his jokes and stories often were the kind that made everyone squirm.

Still, the others didn't let their discomfort show like they had on the first few days. Ijiraq and Tumma often walked away, but Pitu tried to stay patient and hold at least a couple of conversations with Qajaarjuaq each day. None of the conversations addressed the problems they had with one another, and many of their interactions consisted more of Qajaarjuaq insulting the way Pitu did certain tasks, like sharpening his *pana*, his snow knife, or the way Pitu treated his lead dog, Miki.

It took a few more days for the group to be able to work cohesively with the eldest hunter. Qajaarjuaq started to treat Ijiraq and Tumma with more respect and grew interested in teaching Atiq more. The man had even made a small bow out of a caribou antler for the young boy to play with and learn to use, saying that he would also try to make some arrows for him to practise with in the coming days. Qajaarjuaq did not warm up to Pitu, but he was at least being civil. They talked, never comfortably, but their exchanges became less and less the older scolding the younger and more the conversations of equals. Pitu remained patient, though in the middle of the night, Tiri would hear his many complaints about the man.

As they travelled, the signs of wildlife slowly disappeared. They saw no people, no tracks of travelling dog teams. The breathing holes of the seals were frozen over, and the only polar bear tracks they found were long swept over by the wind. Even along the shorelines and hillsides, foxes and hares were nowhere to be found.

The hunters were lucky to have caught multiple seals before they had hit the wasteland, and they planned on saving them for the people who were starving.

Pitu found this lack of wildlife eerily reminiscent of when he'd been lost in the spirit world months ago. It seemed to have been a land abandoned by animals and people, with the creatures of legends reaping whatever was left.

In his bones, he knew that they had not crossed some sort of border into the spirit world. They were still in their own land, far from home, but not that far. Still, he felt uncomfortable. He felt the abandonment of the animals. They had been called away. He knew that he should have expected this, but it was still shocking.

The discomfort was heavy among the hunters. They ate less when they stopped for a bite to eat, rationing their food, just in case. The discomfort was worst for Atiq, who simply couldn't understand the idea of _all_ animals leaving a place. He still had a lot to learn about the responsibilities of hunters and grown-ups, about respecting the animals and spirits as you would respect elders and parents.

There was overwhelming relief among them when they finally spotted a man in the distance. Quickly, they veered their dogs in his direction. As they approached, it became clear that he was standing over a seal hole. There were no dog teams in sight other than their own. His hunting gear was sitting in a bag on the ground, and he was absolutely alone. The man straightened when he saw them, or perhaps heard their approach, and waved his arm for them to come to him.

As they got closer, they could see that he was an old man, his hair long except for the balding top of his head. His cheeks were hollowed. He welcomed them, but his voice was hoarse, and he seemed incredibly tired. Atiq, without asking or being prompted, gave the man a piece of frozen seal that he had cut up early that morning. He had been saving it for a snack during the day.

"Thank you." The old man's voice shook as he took the seal from Atiq. Tumma handed the man a knife to cut the meat into smaller, bite-sized pieces. The old man's hands quavered, but he waved the knife away. He made no move to begin eating the meat that he obviously needed. They watched the old man quietly as he moved to sit down on the ice. The hunters sat on the ice with him. He stared at them, his eyes resting on Pitu. He asked, "A shaman?"

Pitu raised his eyebrows in confirmation. "I've come to help. We brought more seals for your people to eat. Go on, you should eat, too."

The old man's eyes glistened. Without shame, tears fell from the his eyes. "I have not caught a single animal for weeks," he said. "But I can't eat this right now. My empty stomach cannot handle solid food."

The men raised their eyebrows and mumbled some words in understanding. They hadn't thought of that.

"Our caches are all empty, and our children are so hungry. My name is Ka'lak," he continued. "Our shaman died months ago, and we have been struggling since then."

"How far are we from your home?" Pitu asked.

Ka'lak turned slightly and pointed south. "It took me two days of walking to get here. Our dogs were starving, too. We put them out of their suffering, let them free to find their own food. Or we killed the ones that were too long gone."

Pitu could see the heartbreak in Ka'lak's eyes. Though not all hunters would have the same sense of affection for their dogs as Pitu had for Miki, there is no doubt that all hunters felt loyalty to their partners. Life was hard without huskies. They were the most important aspect of hunting because of their strength to haul material and food, their heightened sense of the environment, and their ability to warn of approaching predators.

Pitu sensed another feeling within Ka'lak, one of deep regret and grief. To waste the dogs' deaths would be careless. Pitu knew that they must have eaten the dogs that had died, at least to feed those most in need.

"Let us take you back to your home and your family, Ka'lak," Pitu said, feeling strange calling the old man by his name. Calling those older than himself by their first names always felt odd, and slightly disrespectful. A young person was supposed to address an older person by their relation—uncle, cousin, grandfather, and the like—but Pitu and Ka'lak had no connection that he knew of.

Pitu stood and stretched out his hand toward the old man. Ka'lak took it, his eyes still watering. Pitu guided the old man to his dogsled and made sure he was sitting comfortably on the sled. Atiq joined Ijiraq's dog team, while Tumma helped Qajaarjuaq. They packed the old man's hunting gear and left the deserted hole in the water behind.

The trip was much shorter by dog team. The rest of the journey took less than half the day to finish, and they arrived at the village before the sun had even set. The igluit were all huddled close together, as if gathering for warmth. Pitu knew that this was because the people had recently moved to this area in the hope of finding food. They had built their homes close to each other in a time of great strife, to be able to hear each other's cries, to be able to share the bit of love and laughter they had.

At the sounds of the dogs arriving, several people emerged from their igluit to see who was coming. As soon as they stopped, Pitu and the others hauled off the seals they had caught. They quickly started to share the harvest, handing out pieces of meat to the individuals who came forward. Children tried to eat the food instantly, but they were stopped by their adolescent siblings, who knew that eating it right away would just make them vomit. Teenagers took pieces to elders without hesitation. Mothers with babies on their backs took pieces of meat home to make broth for their families.

Pitu felt a sense of accomplishment at seeing the people take food and go. They had truly been starving. Their faces were sunken and hollow, their skin sickly and pale. Now, they would be having warm, healthy meals. He only wished that they could eat sooner, instead of waiting for the broth to cook.

An elder came forward, an old woman with dark hair. She reminded Pitu of his mother, except for the lack of grey hair. Her eyes were hidden by the folds of her flesh, and her small body was hunched over. She went to Pitu and leaned into him. He embraced her as she wept into the chest of his parka. Her frame was tiny beneath his arms, thin and bony. There was very little talking as the people and Pitu's hunters simply watched. When the old lady let go, she stood on her tiptoes and laid her nose and mouth on Pitu's cheek and, inhaling, gave him a long kunik full of gratitude.

"You've saved us," she sobbed against his face. "You've saved us."

10

Ikuma

After the sun had set, the hunters gathered with elders in the iglu of the leader. It was the woman who had come forward and held onto Pitu. Now, Pitu sat right next to her in the iglu. She would not let go of his hand.

His three hunters and his little brother sat among the other elders. Ka'lak was there, and there were two other elders. The woman holding his hand, Aqiggiq, was telling a story about the shaman who had passed away and left this village in harm's way.

She spoke softly, her voice nearly a whisper. "Last summer, we were well. Our young hunters were good providers, and our babies were healthy. As fall came, our harvesting came less and less, but we were still able to catch enough to live for months. In the dead of winter, just before the sun returned, something happened to our shaman. He became very frightened, and he withdrew from us. He told me that there was nothing he could do to fix what had gone wrong. Not long after, we woke to find his life was gone, drained by the spirits that he had offended."

The other elders mumbled with despondent agreement.

"He did something to disrespect the Woman Below," Ka'lak said, referring to Nuliajuk. "She is angry with him, and her revenge is upon us."

Pitu looked at the hunters. Qajaarjuaq did not seem to be affected by their words, but Tumma and Ijiraq were concerned. Their brows were furrowed, and they kept their heads down to show respect. Pitu looked at his little brother and saw Atiq's wide eyes, frightened.

Inside, Pitu could feel the terror grabbing hold. Since entering the village, and especially since entering this iglu, Pitu had sensed the darkness. Spirits were close—on another plane of existence, but they were here. Unseen, unreachable, but present among them.

"There is another shaman. He is not very far away by dog team," Aqiggiq added. "But he refuses to help us. He said that he was not strong enough. Since then, we have not been eating. Our men travel long and far to find our food, or other hunting parties spare food as they pass us by, but it is rare that we eat enough to live well."

There was a sad pause. Pitu squeezed Aqiggiq's hand reassuringly, as he would squeeze Anaana's with affection. The old woman twisted to look into Pitu's face, her eyes swimming with tears. She added, "We've lost many of our elders. Of the whole village, we're the only elders left who are strong enough to move and walk. Three men and one woman. The rest are bedridden in their igluit."

Pitu spoke his first words since entering the iglu. "I must see the shaman who lives close by," he said. "I can sense the dark spirits. I can sense the pain among them. But I do not know how to speak to them."

As he said this, Pitu looked at Qajaarjuaq and saw disgust on his face. He hesitated to continue, not wanting to share his words in front of the older man and find himself being judged. Though no one said anything, and no one else showed a sense of distrust, he did not think it was wise to say what needed to be said next.

Through the opening of the iglu, Tiri entered. She sat among the people, in the centre of the iglu. Pitu locked eyes with the white fox, and she encouraged him to continue. She assured him that he was safe.

"I don't know how to go to Nuliajuk and appease her," Pitu admitted. "The shaman may be able to help me learn how to do this."

"Yes," Aqiggiq said. She squeezed his hand and continued. "Of course, you are still a learning shaman. Ka'lak can take you to him."

Qajaarjuaq blew out a deep breath, a sigh of annoyance. The elders didn't seem to hear his disrespect. It was only obvious to Pitu and the other hunters because they knew Qajaarjuaq. Pitu stared at him pointedly, but Qajaarjuaq avoided the eye contact. Tumma and Ijiraq had clearly heard it and were now also looking at Qajaarjuaq.

"Thank you for welcoming us into your homes," Pitu said finally. Aqiggiq squeezed his hand once more with affection. "We should rest. All of us. We can talk more tomorrow."

They started leaving the iglu. Pitu was last to leave, and before he crawled out, Aqiggiq said, "We are thankful you've come, young shaman. It is a shame that this will change you so."

Pitu turned to look at her. She was tearful again. "What do you mean?"

The tears fell from her eyes. "You cannot go to Nuliajuk and come back the same man that you were. You cannot appease these spirits without losing a part of yourself."

His thoughts went straight to Taktuq, his improbable friend. The old shaman had been so lost and broken. Would Pitu end up like him after all? Would they walk down the same path?

"Perhaps I will change," Pitu said, thinking deeply and carefully, "but there are many people who will try to bring me back and who care for me. If I change, I hope that they can help me overcome it."

"I will hope for that," Aqiggiq said. "I will hope to have you return as you are now."

He thanked her a final time and left the iglu. Outside, the three hunters stood with Atiq, waiting for Pitu to tell them what to do. They had built themselves some igluit shortly after arriving. The hunters were silent. Pitu was not surprised.

"We'll help the people tomorrow with chores while they regain their strength and fill their empty stomachs," Pitu said. "The day after, I must go to see the shaman with Ka'lak. Atiq will come with me, but I need another one of you to accompany me. The other two will stay and continue to help this camp get back on their feet."

Tumma, almost instantly, volunteered to go with him. They all agreed and went into their igluit to sleep. As soon as Atiq's head fell upon the warmth and softness of the caribou skins, he began to snore.

Pitu stayed up, thinking of Qajaarjuaq. He wanted the eldest of their hunting party to come, so that Pitu could keep a close watch on him. He didn't trust Qajaarjuaq, and he didn't want Qajaarjuaq's presence to disturb the camp as they were rehabilitating. The people were vulnerable, and Qajaarjuaq was a man who took advantage of vulnerable people.

Still, he was relieved he would have a break from the man. Pitu felt bad for Ijiraq. He had to make sure to talk to Ijiraq before leaving to ensure that he would keep a close eye on Qajaarjuaq. A part of him was sure that having Qajaarjuaq on the day trip would be harmful in some way. The feeling was echoed by the spirits.

Eventually, Pitu's worrying slowed. He fell asleep.

Pitu's sleep was heavy and full of vivid dreams. He followed Tiri along the floe edge on a beautiful, sunny day. The breeze was soft, carrying the voices of the spirits. They encouraged him to drink in the light, to store it within himself.

The sky was the bluest hue, and the ice was pure white. The sun beating down should have blinded Pitu, but he did not have to squint. He didn't need his antler sunglasses. He simply walked and took in the beauty.

A whale basked in the water, and terns rested upon the surface of the sea. A seal would emerge occasionally, popping its head out of the ocean to watch the human on the ice.

Tiri continued walking along the edge of the ice. It was solid and sturdy. Pitu walked farther from the edge, afraid that a piece might break under his weight and he would drown. Time was slow, and the two walked for quite a while before stopping at a large crack in the ice. Sculpins swam leisurely between the chunks of ice.

The fox looked at the crevasse, then back at Pitu. Before him, Pitu could see a pair of footprints leading into the watery crack in the ice.

The weather changed. The sun was hidden by a drifting cloud. Pitu shivered in the shade. The animals in the open water dove under the surface. Only the sculpins stayed the same. In fact, more emerged from the depths of the ocean.

On the other side of the crack, an owl landed. Its feathers were white with delicately placed black spots. Its eyes were a shade of yellow reminiscent of summer flowers. The owl flapped its wings for a moment, then tilted its head, looking at Pitu. *What would an owl be doing at the floe?* Pitu thought. *There are no lemmings for it to eat here.*

The two stared at one another, a silent conversation between spirits. Pitu knew that he was supposed to learn something from this owl, but thoughts escaped him. The dream had been so pleasant before the owl arrived.

The owl stretched its legs, flapped its wings again, then took flight once more. Pitu tracked its soaring path. He realized that he hadn't looked backward toward land, only forward toward the floe edge. Now, he watched as the owl flew toward a mountain close by. It dove back down at the base of the mountain.

He felt his eyes grow heavy, and he heard a woman's voice ominously whisper, *"Soon, young shaman."*

Pitu woke with the woman's voice ringing in his head. It was an elegant voice that held power. He could only assume it belonged to Nuliajuk. Pitu felt a great weight within his body, a weight of fatigue and paralyzing fear. It took him a long time to open his eyes, as if they were weighed down the way water weighed down wet clothing. When he finally managed it, his little brother was not in bed. Pitu must have slept for a long time if the boy had left the iglu without him.

Slowly, Pitu began to fully wake. He sat up and rubbed his eyes, then his face. The owl from his dream confused him. The floe edge, with its abundance of animals, made sense with Nuliajuk's call to him, but the owl was out of place.

It took great effort for Pitu to put on his parka and caribou-skin pants. He could have stretched and yawned until time stopped, but time never stopped for him. He finally left the iglu to see how the others were doing.

Outside, the world was quiet. A few children were playing games of little activity. They were playing guessing games on the outskirts of the village while teenage girls—their older sisters, undoubtedly—sat in the snow and watched them in boredom. Pitu looked around for adults, but there were few people nearby. He noticed that the dog teams were gone. He assumed they had been taken for a hunting trip.

Pitu approached the teenage girls. Their backs were toward him, and for a moment he hesitated, his memories going back to when he had approached qallupilluit in the other world. At the sounds of his footsteps, though, the girls turned. Their faces were human, shy smiles planted upon their lips.

"Ai," Pitu said. "Where is everyone?"

Some of the girls hid their faces in their hands, too shy to speak to him. They were not much younger than he was. Shyness ran strong among young girls. Pitu used to be shy as well, and he used to struggle with talking to girls other than Saima. He realized how easily he had just asked the girls his question, and how hard that would have been for him a year ago. Quiet confidence grew within him as he thought this.

One of the girls looked pointedly at Pitu. She had tattoos on her face and seemed to be older than the others. She wore a simple yet not well-made caribou-skin amauti, with no extravagant designs and a small hood. He recognized that the simplicity of her clothing's design meant that she was an orphan. By the fade of her tattoos it looked as though she had had them for a long time. It was a rare practice, but sometimes if a girl was orphaned at a young age, she was tattooed—a mark of maturity and readiness for marriage—in an effort to have her married sooner.

"An elder has died. They are gathering on the other side of that hill," she said, pointing to a small rise in the land close by. Now that Pitu knew where to look, he could see the dog team's tracks rounding the hill. The girl added, "I can walk with you, if you wish."

Pitu agreed, and the girl stood. It wouldn't be a very long walk, and something in his gut told him that he should befriend this girl. Pitu's parents had always told him to treat orphans with respect. They were often mistreated by the community, especially if they had been very young when they lost their parents. It was hard enough to provide for your own family. If there was anything to spare, the orphans were given only scraps of both food and fur. If they lost their parents when they were very young and had not been trained to sew, build their own iglu, or hunt, they were given secondhand or damaged clothing and made to sleep in the chill of the ice porches, or with the dogs. Pitu was taught that orphans were strong people who had survived great loss, and their advice was invaluable.

Another part of Pitu's gut told him that she was beautiful. He tried to ignore it.

"My name is Piturniq," he said as they walked. They were far enough away from the snow houses now that their conversation wouldn't be overheard, if they were to have a conversation, that is. So far, they hadn't spoken since he agreed that they should walk together.

"I am Ikuma," she said. She hesitated before she smiled. Her voice had been easy-going, and her smile was soft as summer air. He could see the tattoos faded underneath her dark skin. They stretched as she smiled. The tattoos looked much older than Saima's, but she herself seemed to be the same age. Pitu wondered if the effort of tattooing her so much younger than usual had its desired outcome of marriage. After a moment of silence, she said, "You slept very late, Shaman."

Pitu was slightly upset that she called him by his title rather than his name. He also understood why. Calling someone in his role by their name was disrespectful. Though he had told her his name, she still knew that it would be wrong to use it. They followed the path of the dog teams. The wake of the team left the snow upturned. They walked alongside it, where the snow was smooth and hard enough to carry their weight without breaking.

"I must have been tired," Pitu replied. "Our journey was long."

He shook his head in discomfort. What a terrible conversation. He didn't know what to say.

She giggled quietly, then said, "It's good for you to be well rested if you are to be the one who saves us from the spirits that haunt our people."

Pitu was slightly taken aback by this. He asked her, "Do you know a lot about these spirits?"

"My grandfather was the shaman who was here before." Her voice became quiet. "He told me that they were coming before . . . before he died."

Pitu felt the urge to touch her, to console her. He almost reached out, but then thought better of it. They didn't know each other very well, and a consoling gesture might not be so comforting from a stranger.

When he looked at her face, though, it was not sadness he saw. It was relief. He asked her, "Are you glad he is gone?"

She looked at him with an apologetic expression, but there was no denial in it. She answered, "My grandfather was not a good man."

Pitu raised his eyebrows. He was lucky to have a caring family. Not everyone had that.

"Do you have any other family here?" he asked.

"Just my grandmother," she replied. Ikuma shrugged, looking back at him. Their eyes locked for a moment. Pitu felt an urge of longing, something he had only felt with one other person. She added, "My parents passed away when I was a little girl."

"I hope you are safe here," he mumbled.

Her expression faltered. They were rounding the hillside now. At the bottom of the hill, there were broken icebergs along the coastline. Pitu avoided the ice, not wanting to think of the qallupilluit again. Even though these icebergs were completely normal, something he encountered every day of his life, he couldn't shake off his memories. He could feel the dark spirits in this place lurking close by. They were the cause of his fear.

As they rounded the hill, they could see the people and the dogs gathered. This area had less snow, a little valley where the wind swept the snow away. The men had dug up rocks from the ground. Pitu could see mounds of rocks throughout the area, graves dotting the land. Now they piled another mound.

At their arrival, the gatherers looked up. Some smiled; some showed no emotion. Tumma and Ijiraq were there helping, greeting Pitu's arrival. Qajaarjuaq grimaced, but Pitu chose to ignore him. Atiq came up to Pitu and Ikuma and said, "I tried to wake you, big brother."

"It's okay," Pitu said. He could tell that some of the people were unhappy with Pitu's tardy arrival, interrupting a funeral. Now that he was here, he realized he should have stayed at camp.

Aqiggiq, the old lady who led this camp, came to greet Pitu. She spoke loudly enough for the others to hear her. "I trust that you have good reasons for your long rest."

Pitu raise his eyebrows in agreement. Ikuma had retreated, her head meekly hanging from her neck. She was afraid of the others here. An urge to protect her swept over Pitu.

"I am sorry for the loss," Pitu said. "Perhaps my journey to see and learn from the other shaman will be sooner rather than later."

Aqiggiq bobbed her head as she distractedly murmured, "Mhmm . . ." She eyed Ikuma, seeming unimpressed with the girl. The look was fleeting, only twisting her face for the slightest second, but Pitu had caught it. Aqiggiq said, "Come, Shaman." She took hold of Pitu's arm. "Ikuma, you can return to camp now. Aren't there children to look after?"

Ikuma, still looking at her feet, raised her eyebrows and began to turn back to where they had come from. Pitu said, "Thank you for bringing me, Ikuma. I will not forget your help."

She stopped for a moment and half-turned to look at him. The barest smile graced her face. Her eyes lit up. She said nothing, but she closed her eyes in a silent gesture of appreciation. Ikuma left, and Pitu had the urge not to let her out of his sight.

He looked away. Aqiggiq looked at Pitu through squinting eyes, then shook her head in annoyance. "That girl has no manners," the elder said. "She was not raised right."

"Perhaps growing up without parents makes one not prone to manners," Pitu replied firmly, his words carrying a bit of admonishment at the elder's cruelty. Aqiggiq looked away from him, embarrassed. He added, "Perhaps she knows when it matters and when it doesn't."

A little taken aback, she raised her eyebrows high, wrinkling her forehead even more than usual. In an attempt to save face, she quickly said, "Yes, yes, of course. Yes, we do try to help her."

Guilt swept over Pitu. The protective feelings he had rapidly developed for Ikuma had led him to say these things. Pitu touched Aqiggiq's arm. "Yes, I am sure she is thankful for the help she receives," he said.

"I do have a soft spot for orphans. My little brother here is one."

Aqiggiq looked at Atiq, her eyes softening at the sight of the little boy. "Oh, you look so alike. I did not know he was adopted."

Pitu chose not to dwell on the way Aqiggiq felt about Ikuma. Sometimes habits lived so easily in one's soul that the person could no longer see how things looked to an outsider. Perhaps her cruelty toward Ikuma had been a part of her life for too long, so long that she no longer interpreted it as being unkind, but as a normal way to treat and interact with the orphaned girl. Pitu looked at his little brother. It was lucky indeed that Atiq had been adopted, and therefore did not have to endure the kind of hardships that many orphans did. Pitu, too, was adopted, but he still had a close relationship with his birth parents. A lot of adopted children stayed close to their birth families, but Atiq had no relatives other than those he was adopted into.

He'd be sure to see Ikuma later to let her know that she could find a friendship with him. Maybe he'd even offer to bring her back to his village.

Pitu paid his respects to the buried elder. He looked at all the graves, most of them recently made. Some were short, some long, and some heartbreakingly tiny. For the most part, those who had been unhappy with Pitu's late arrival seemed to have let it go. They welcomed him in their grief. Qajaarjuaq was the only one who had no warm feelings for him.

After the burial, the hunters brought the people back to camp on their dog teams. Aqiggiq walked back between Pitu and Atiq, her arms intertwined with theirs. She was strong for a little old lady, surprisingly so. They hardly spoke to one another, but their earlier spat seemed long forgotten.

As they approached camp, Aqiggiq finally spoke. She had not been emotional during the burial of the elder, and now was no different. She was a strong woman, and she spoke with a level voice. Calmly, she said, "You have already done good in our community. You have fed us. We are very thankful."

She took her arm from Atiq's and reached out to touch Pitu's hand. He could feel the appreciation in that touch, even through their thick mitts. He pressed his lips into a tight smile.

Atiq, almost instantly, took the opportunity to run away. He left to join the other children. They were still playing games that weren't rowdy, so as not to disturb the grieving. Pitu remembered Atiq's boredom when they had been caught in the blizzard earlier in their trip. It had been annoying at the time, but now Pitu took comfort in seeing his little brother take advantage of being around other children. Atiq sat with the kids as they built tiny villages in the snow.

Aqiggiq let go of Pitu, and they said a final few words before she returned to her own iglu. Pitu looked at the faces of those outside, looking for Ikuma. She was nowhere in sight.

Qajaarjuaq came to Pitu, a grimace lining his face deeply. *He looks twisted*, Pitu thought. *Twisted so tight that his skin might rip.*

"Good sleep, Angakkuq?" Qajaarjuaq said, spitting the title out as usual. "Yeah, it must have been a good sleep. You must be so tired from all the hard *work* you do."

Pitu knew that Qajaarjuaq wouldn't listen if he tried to explain or defend himself. He felt no urge to reply anyway. He walked away from Qajaarjuaq. He was thankful that the other man didn't follow him, but he heard Qajaarjuaq mumble harsh words as they parted. Pitu paid no mind.

He spent the rest of the day visiting the sick elders, bedridden in their igluit. Ijiraq and Tumma stayed busy helping the other hunters cut up and prepare the meat they had brought. Pitu didn't worry himself over Qajaarjuaq.

The elders, though weak and close to death, were happy to have his company. Each of them held onto Pitu's hands and hoarsely spoke of how his mere presence uplifted them. Some of the elders were ancient people with lines wrinkled deep into their skin, their flesh folded over and droopy. These elders, so old that their jaws could hardly move and their vocal chords were almost withered away, praised Pitu with sincerity.

One of them, an ancient old man named Nassak, spoke in a quiet voice. Pitu had to lean down, his face close enough that the two were breathing each other in. He told stories of his childhood, of hunting for his family, and his experiences with other shamans in his life. Pitu could tell that the elder was thinking about his life as if it were finished, as if he would never wake up again after this moment. By the way he looked, Pitu couldn't help but echo the old man's feelings. Pitu gave him broth in the pauses of his stories. Nassak had lived a good life.

He saw more people, young and old. He talked to the people and heard their stories. In return, they asked him to tell his own stories. Pitu obliged, telling them of the spirit world. The people enjoyed hearing of the joys of running with the northern lights and the giant that lived with her animals.

The last iglu he visited was the home of an elderly lady and her granddaughter. He recognized Ikuma instantly, and he felt his heart begin drumming a new song. The old lady moaned in a dazed half-sleep, awake but not quite there. Ikuma invited Pitu to sit close to her grandmother. The old woman opened her eyes when Pitu sat down. She reached for him, calling a name that he didn't know.

Ikuma translated. "She thinks you're my grandfather."

Her grandmother spoke again, her voice full of pain. "Why have you done this, my husband? Why have you done this?"

Pitu felt her agony. It was not just illness—she was sick from lack of nutrition, but there were deeper wounds within her. He could see the abuse of her soul. He could feel it in her breath. She did not cry. She simply asked the question, over and over again. Pitu did not answer; there was nothing he could say.

He grabbed hold of her hand, as he had with all the other sick elders he had visited that day. Ikuma's grandmother held on weakly. Pitu looked over at Ikuma. She tended a qulliq, keeping the light and warmth in the iglu. Her hair was tucked into her parka, but loose tresses fell from her braid to frame her face. Even in the dim light of the qulliq, he could see her tattoos.

When Pitu looked back to the grandmother, she was sleeping soundly. He stroked his thumb against her hand, willing that her dreams were soft and warm.

He looked back to Ikuma, who stared at her grandmother with affection. Her brows wrinkled with worry. She spoke without looking at him, her eyes focused solely on her grandmother. "She has been sick the longest of all the elders. Since before my grandfather died. But she hasn't passed away. I think she clings to life for me."

Ikuma spoke truth. Pitu could feel it in the air, in the few good spirits that were trying to help this village against the dark. Her grandmother couldn't bear the thought of leaving her granddaughter alone among these people. It was because of their respect for the old lady alone that the people took care of the girl, giving her scraps of food and fur to survive.

Pitu let go of the grandmother's hand, feeling that she was calm enough to sleep well for a day or two. There wasn't much else an elder as sick as she could do but sleep. He scooted over to sit closer to Ikuma. He asked her, "Do you have any friends here?"

Ikuma looked away from her grandmother, her eyes meeting Pitu's now. They began to well up, then she wiped the tears away with her sleeve. She scrunched her nose. "My parents died before I could even remember them. My grandmother spoiled me, so I didn't learn how to sew very well. My grandparents were much older than most. They had no patience for teaching, and our camp has always struggled with providing enough food for everyone."

There was neglect written into her skin, just as there was abuse written into her grandmother. When people were concerned for their own family's wellbeing, looking after another person who couldn't help themselves was an added stress. He could see that Ikuma understood why she had been mistreated. There was little patience among this community; little patience to teach a girl how to sew when she was crying for her mother. They had given her those tattoos at a young age so that she could be married off into a family. That plan had fallen through, or else there would be another man in this iglu with them.

"Tomorrow I am leaving for a couple of days," Pitu told her, feeling obliged to her in some way. There was so little love for her here. "When I return, when this camp has the animals back, I want you to come back to my home with me. My mother can help you."

Ikuma took her eyes off Pitu and looked back at her grandmother. Solemnly, she said, "I cannot leave her."

Pitu grabbed hold of Ikuma's hand. He didn't know what he wanted to do. Emotions were running within him and making his mind blurry. For a fleeting second, he thought of Saima. Her lovely laugh and her mischievous grin. He looked at Ikuma. He saw in her someone who had experienced terrible hardship, but who might one day smile brightly with the aid of patience and friendship. With love.

He let go. They had only met today. He shouldn't have promised her such things. Pitu stood up, saying, "I have to go. I must see you when I come back from my journey."

For a moment, Ikuma said nothing. She looked only at Pitu's feet. He waited for her to say something. When it seemed that she had nothing to say, he took a step backward, turning to leave. "Safe journey," Ikuma said finally, her voice thick. "Please come back." Pitu left. He thought of the night he and Saima had stayed up late talking. She had asked him to return safely, too.

He stayed up late, unable to sleep. His heart raced as he thought of Ikuma. When he eventually fell asleep, his dreams swam with her image before changing to the faces of the spirits and creatures he had grown to know so well.

11

Ukpik

In the wee hours of morning, Ijiraq and Tumma entered the iglu where Atiq and Pitu slept. They left Atiq sleeping while Tumma shook Pitu awake. Pitu opened his heavy eyes, groggy with the interruption of the sleep that had taken him so long to achieve. He groaned, feeling—for the first time in a very long time—like a teenager again. He'd forgotten what it was like.

"Piturniq," Tumma whispered. "What are we going to do about Qajaarjuaq?"

Pitu opened his eyes wide, the question fully waking him up. He sat up quickly, causing a head rush. "What did he do now?"

Tumma shrugged. "Nothing yet. But we leave today, and you have to talk to him."

Pitu rubbed his eyes. "I know," he moaned, drawling out the word. He was beginning to remind himself of Atiq's annoying complaints of boredom. Pitu stopped whining. He looked directly at Ijiraq. "I will talk to him before we leave, but you will still have to keep an eye on him. There is little chance he will listen to anything I say."

Ijiraq raised his eyebrows, having already known this. "He won't listen to me, either."

"As long as you're here to stop his bad behaviours," Pitu said. The others agreed. Pitu was glad that they all understood. "I think that is all we can do."

They left it at that. Pitu got dressed and woke Atiq. The four of them ate a dent into a piece of caribou thigh before heading outside into the morning with the rising sun. Tumma and Atiq left to find Ka'lak, the elder who would help them find the shaman. They would get started on preparing the supplies for the journey, while Pitu and Ijiraq went to find Qajaarjuaq.

It didn't take long. Qajaarjuaq was fast asleep within his iglu, and a woman was inside with him. She tended a qulliq while Qajaarjuaq's snoring shook the snow house. Pitu had expected to find the man alone and felt embarrassed to see a woman there. His eyes widened and he quickly backed out of the snow house, bumping into Ijiraq on the way out. Pitu thought this might have been funny if he hadn't felt so embarrassed. Not knowing the reason they had backed out, Ijiraq asked, "What's wrong?"

Pitu said nothing. He and Ijiraq waited outside for a moment before the woman emerged in her parka. Wordlessly and quickly, she left.

Inside, Qajaarjuaq had awoken to the commotion. He was sitting up in bed by the time Pitu and Ijiraq returned. The man's strong arms were crossed over his bare chest, his long hair falling across his shoulders and biceps. There were scars on Qajaarjuaq's chest, the cause of which must have been painful. "What do you want?" Qajaarjuaq asked, annoyed and unimpressed. "Aren't you leaving today, _Angakkuq_?"

Pitu was mustering up a patient reply, but Ijiraq held up a hand. Ijiraq's expression had changed, annoyance morphed into frustration. His brows were so deeply furrowed that the space between them was almost gone. "How can you be so shameless?" Ijiraq said. "You act like you are better than us, yet you are about as useful as a dull knife."

Pitu was overcome with admiration at the insult. He wished he could have come up with something as clever as that. It was something Saima would say. However, he also knew that these words were not going to help the situation. He expected a reaction of violence from Qajaarjuaq, but the man simply said,

"At least a dull knife can still cut. You just have to push harder."

"Qajaarjuaq," Pitu said, trying to change the course of the conversation. He was beginning to feel uncomfortable leaving these two behind for a couple of days. "I've told you before that we need to talk about the problems we're having so that they do not affect the people we are trying to help. From the very beginning of this trip, we have known that our purpose is to help these people, and you have acted like a spoiled child the whole time.

"I am leaving today to try to meet Nuliajuk and appease her," Pitu continued. "I am the leader of our hunting group. You have caused too much stress among this group, even worrying my little brother. You have disrespected my authority the entire trip. If you continue, I will be forced to send you back to our camp—to your father—with shame and consequence."

Silence followed Pitu's clear expression of his displeasure. Qajaarjuaq, a sneer still drawn on his face, simply blinked back at Pitu. Ijiraq looked at Pitu, reflecting back the same admiration that had been on Pitu's face earlier. Pitu's wasn't a clever remark, but it had grit.

Qajaarjuaq wrinkled his nose, his mouth twisting as he said, "A child cannot tell a man what to do."

Ijiraq again spoke before Pitu knew what to say. "Who do you think the child is here? Piturniq? It's you. You act as one."

"Why do you speak for Piturniq?" Qajaarjuaq lashed out sharply. "Don't you know he sleeps with your wife?"

Pitu felt his heartbeat speed up. His head began to throb as blood rushed through his body. He felt as though his chest was shrinking inward, like he was closing into himself with the guilt and shame. Ijiraq's shoulders drooped, but the words didn't seem to affect him as much as they had Pitu.

"My wife tells me everything," Ijiraq said, his voice shaky. "I knew when she went to speak to Piturniq. I trust him to be a good man. You are so clouded by your own depravity that you think all men do what you would."

Qajaarjuaq leapt from the bed, only needing one step before he could reach Ijiraq and hurt him. Pitu acted quickly, jumping between the two. This did not stop Qajaarjuaq from throwing punches. The older man's fist landed on Pitu's cheek, while the other hand reached around to grab Ijiraq. Qajaarjuaq must have known that Pitu would jump out.

Instinct drove Pitu forward. He shoved Qajaarjuaq away, then turned and shoved Ijiraq in the opposite direction. He went back to Qajaarjuaq and pinned the older man down. Qajaarjuaq seemed surprised by Pitu's strength. He didn't know the ways a shaman must train and continue training to keep his physical form as strong as his spirit.

Pitu's voice shook as he said, "Only weak men act the way you do. That is why you will never be a leader."

Pitu pushed himself away from Qajaarjuaq. The older man seemed stunned—no quick reply, no violent outburst. Pitu gave Ijiraq a look, a leave-us-alone-for-a-minute look. Ijiraq left the iglu.

"I know you have little tolerance or respect for me," Pitu said in a low voice, "but it will do you good to remember that I am more than a child. I have the spirits on my side."

With that, he left. Pitu didn't know if his words would have any effect on Qajaarjuaq, but he did have a sense that the physical confrontation did more to persuade him than anything else.

Outside the iglu, life carried on. As the people of the village had begun to regain strength from the meals they were eating, their small joys were returning as well. Children played outside—still not as actively as in most villages, but they played nonetheless. Women cooed and sang to their babies, and men flirted with their wives. Pitu could feel their growing comfort in life again. The community would have been surprised to learn of the tension within that iglu.

Ijiraq was waiting for Pitu. When he crawled out of the iglu, Ijiraq didn't say anything. His mouth was pressed into a tight line. Nervousness shot through Pitu as he remembered what Qajaarjuaq had said inside. Ijiraq had handled the outburst calmly, but now that they were alone, Pitu didn't know what to expect.

When Ijiraq remained silent, Pitu said the only words he could think of. "I should have made her leave my iglu that night."

"Yes. You should have," he said curtly. Ijiraq shook his head, as if shaking the thoughts from his mind. He added, "There are always times when we know we should do what is right but cannot help but do what we want. I just wish Saima wasn't always doing whatever she wanted. I wish she had thought of me when she chose to visit you."

Pitu looked at Ijiraq with great remorse. He could imagine the future, once Tagaaq was long gone, with Ijiraq leading the camp. Pitu would be the shaman, advising Ijiraq and consulting with the spirits, but Ijiraq's wisdom was infinite. Pitu knew that Ijiraq was angry and embarrassed, but the calm the other man exhibited was unwavering.

What could he say? Pitu bowed his head slightly, a gesture full of both gratitude and apology. "I am sorry. I cannot change what happened, but you have become a good friend of mine, and my only excuse is that I did not know you as I do now."

Ijiraq raised his eyebrows, still upset but focusing on the tasks ahead. He said, "You should head out soon, before Qajaarjuaq recovers from his wounded pride. The food we brought is already starting to run low. This village needs the animals to return."

With that, Pitu agreed and said his goodbyes to Ijiraq. Pitu raised his hand for Ijiraq to shake. He was relieved when the other man took it in his, a small smile on his face. "Good luck," Ijiraq said, before they went their separate ways.

Pitu met up with Tumma, Atiq, and Ka'lak. The four of them continued to gather their supplies for the journey. They made sure they had extra rope and harpoon heads, and a little bit of extra food to offer the shaman they were off to visit.

Just before they were about to leave, Aqiggiq came to say her farewell. She hugged and kissed the hunters and wished them luck.

Out on the flat ice of the ocean, Ka'lak pointed toward a range of hills not quite tall enough to be called mountains. Among those hills, he said, the shaman lived alone.

"Why does he live alone?" Tumma asked.

Pitu knew the answer before Ka'lak replied. "To find peace."

There were many stories of shamans leaving their communities to find peace. It was what Taktuq had done. Pitu, still young and new to the spirits, didn't quite understand it. Even alone, a shaman is constantly visited by the spirits, constantly audience to their fancy. Was it the humans that they needed peace from?

It didn't take long to reach the range of hills. By the number of tracks in the snow, it looked like the animal life in this place was more abundant than in the village. *We must be close to a floe edge,* Pitu thought. He slowed his dog team, the others doing the same.

"Look at the tracks," Pitu said, pointing at the windswept prints. He asked Ka'lak, "Did you come to hunt here?"

Ka'lak looked at the snow. "What tracks?" he replied.

Pitu looked at the other two. Tumma and Atiq didn't seem to see them either. Pitu shook his head, dismissing what he'd said. The prints were not animal tracks; they were the paths of spirits. "Never mind," he said. "I must be tired."

"We tried hunting here," Ka'lak added, "but there is nothing. The shaman says it is because he lives alone that the animals do not come."

They continued on. The sky was clouded over with patches of blue, the wind on the ice strong but not troubling. Amid the range of hills, Pitu could see a single high peak, the rock of the lone mountain peeking from beneath the snow. He was sure that this hill, tallest among the others, was their destination. In a way, he felt as though he recognized it.

They stopped once more to let the dogs rest and to eat a little hearty meal of seal. Pitu didn't know what to expect. The only other shaman he had met since he learned his true nature had been an old man hiding in fear. An old man who had lived alone within the spirit world for decades. What would it be like to meet a shaman in the world of the living?

Still, this shaman lived alone, a hermit among Inuit. How different would he be from Taktuq? Pitu thought.

Very soon, Pitu would be learning how to dive into the ocean, swimming to meet Nuliajuk. He had never even tried swimming in a little pond, let alone the frigid, ice-covered sea.

He thought of the story of Nuliajuk. A young woman who had many men propose marriage to her. A young woman with a heart that could not be persuaded by men. She had lived alone with her father, at a camp far from others. Men would come, one after another, to ask to be her husband. Word of her legendary beauty had spread throughout the land. She refused every man who asked to marry her.

Nuliajuk's father had grown tired of providing for his picky daughter. He asked her to say yes to a proposal, to help them survive in the harshness of the world—in the harshness of the weather and the environment, and the spirits. Nuliajuk considered her father's plea. When the next man came, a strange man of beauty as great as hers, she accepted. He had promised her a home of great abundance and luxury. Soon, they travelled across the sea to his home on a small island in the middle of the ocean.

She found no beauty in the island, which was nothing more than a shale shoreline with little vegetation or protection from the salty wind of the sea. There was no *qarmaq*, no house made of rock, sod, whale bone, and caribou skin. As Nuliajuk walked the island, she tripped over a nest-like area made from fish bones, covered in feathers and fish skin. She looked toward her husband, but the man had transformed. He stood, no longer a handsome man, but a half-fulmar creature. Long white feathers grew from his arms. His nose and mouth stretched outward like a beak. She could see a grin among his features, his eyes alight with mischief. "You married a bird, my dearest wife," the fulmar-man said. "Did you know that?"

Nuliajuk cried for her father to come and save her, but the wind was strong, and her voice wasn't carried far. She cried all the time, and her husband found mirth in her sorrow.

There was a day, however, when her husband had left to catch fish. She cried again for her father, and the wind carried her voice to his camp with sweet yet cunning care. Her father heard her unmistakable cry, and he sped to her on his qajaq. He found her crying among fish bones, and he took her away from that place. She held onto the qajaq as he paddled across the ocean.

The fulmar returned from his hunt and found the island without his beautiful wife. Angered by her leaving, the fulmar rose into the sky and spotted Nuliajuk on her father's qajaq. He swooped down, flapping his wings to create a stronger wind. A storm brewed beneath his powerful wings. "If you let her go," the fulmar called to Nuliajuk's father, "I will let you live."

By then, Nuliajuk's father had grown terrified of the huge waves swelling into them. He shivered as cold water drenched through his clothing and swam into his skin. His terror, so strong, caused him to push his daughter into the terrible sea beneath the boat.

But . . . Nuliajuk held onto the boat. She held tight and strong. She clung there, as her fingers turned white. The fulmar spoke again, "If you let her go, I will let you live."

Nuliajuk's father grabbed his knife made of sharpened ivory. He raised the knife, and he plunged it down into the side of the qajaq, cutting through Nuliajuk's fingers at the first knuckle. As her fingertips fell into the sea, they transformed into creatures. Seals and fish.

Still, she clung to the qajaq with her half-fingers.

Again, her father heard the fulmar's cry: "If you let her go, I will let you live."

Again, he raised his knife. He plunged it into her hands and cut her fingers at her second knuckles.

The stubs of her fingers fell into the ocean, and again they transformed into creatures. Walruses and belugas.

Nuliajuk finally lost her grip and, unable to swim, she sank beneath the waves, drifting to the bottom.

As she drifted down, Nuliajuk did not drown. She did not die. Instead, she transformed, just as her fingers had. She sank to the bottom of the sea. She breathed. She protected her new children.

Respect was due to Nuliajuk, always and forever. Through her tragedy, new life was brought into the world. Any broken taboo, any disrespect or irresponsibility, could cause enormous damage to the people's livelihood. Hunters and families were entirely dependent on the ocean, on the animals that Nuliajuk birthed. If she became offended, she called them back to her.

Pitu thought of her, of how frightening the story was. In a way, he believed that at the bottom of the sea, he would see her. In another, he didn't believe it. Though he had seen power, though he had seen greatness and the seeming impossibility of spirits, he still had trouble believing one could travel beneath the sea. No one could hold their breath long enough, and no one could breathe underwater.

Still, he had to try. He had to help those people, starving in the slow melt of spring.

They slowed down as the mouth of a cave became discernible among the rocks of the lone mountain. In the light of the sun, it only seemed to be a shadow among the boulders and pack ice bunched up on the shoreline. Pitu squinted and thought that perhaps he could see the flickering light of a lit stone lamp inside.

The lone mountain seemed more like a jagged cliff, rising toward the clouds. Pitu could imagine birds nestled into the nooks and crannies, warming their eggs and diving into the summer water that would surround this area. He wondered where the shaman would go once the ice melted.

Though the dogs obeyed the hunters' calls for them to stop, they were unhappy. They cried and struggled against their harnesses. They fought each other. Atiq tried to feed the dogs, but none of them would eat.

Ka'lak guided Pitu to the cave. Tumma and Atiq stayed with the dogs, attempting to calm them. With each step closer, Pitu's apprehension grew. He understood the uneasiness of the dog teams. He felt the strangeness of this place. Still, Ka'lak led Pitu into the cave.

Inside, the light from the flames was faint. The two followed the lamp's glow. As they rounded a jagged stone wall, Ka'lak stopped. He urged Pitu forward. Pitu stepped into the light of the cave. A figure sat quietly, solemn, on a bed made from lemming skins sewn together. Layer upon layer, hundreds of lemming skins made a patchwork of blankets. Each skin was the size of the sole of one of Pitu's *kamiik*. The figure, seeming not to have noticed Pitu and Ka'lak's arrival, had its hood drawn up over its head.

The figure looked up at Pitu, and he knew instantly that this was neither a man nor a shaman. Pitu turned slightly, and he said to Ka'lak, "You may go back outside. Help Tumma and Atiq calm the dogs."

Without a word, Ka'lak nodded and left. Pitu turned back to the creature that the villagers called a shaman. He could understand their mistake. To any unknowing eye, this creature appeared to be a human wearing an elegant white parka with decorative feathers. It wore a white mask over its face, slits carved into the eyes to allow it to see. A black beak protruded from the mask, making it resemble an owl.

"So, you visited my dream the night before last," Pitu addressed the spirit. The spirit tilted its head, an eerie gesture coming from a masked creature. Pitu continued, "I had wondered why an owl would appear at a floe edge."

"So young you are," the spirit said, its voice sounding ambiguously human, neither female nor male, neither young nor old. "So young, and they send you to the sea?"

The Owl did not wait for an answer. "Yet within your youth there is age and wisdom," it continued. "So much experience within your soul. Is it true you killed a qallupilluq? Yes, it must be. The spirits would not talk of such horrendous things if they were untrue, even considering how bored we get. So well you are respected among the humans, and so well you are respected among the spirits. You must rival with the sun for the love all creatures have for you."

As the Owl spoke, Pitu took in his surroundings. The remnants of lemmings were scattered throughout the cave. Tiny, delicate bones littered the ground, discarded or decorative, Pitu did not know. There were other animal parts, too. The bones and skins of seals and fish and birds were strewn about. Most surprising and interesting of all, masks of various styles, each made from different materials and representing a different animal, perched on hangers carved into the stone walls of the cave.

The Owl's voice drifted to a lull, following Pitu's gaze to the masks. Soon, the Owl's voice quickened once more as it spoke,

"Ah, yes, the masks . . .

The masks . . .

Do you like my masks?"

Pitu raised his eyebrows in agreement. He'd never seen a mask before, but he had heard stories of them. Masks that brought spirits into the physical world. Masks that took humans into the spirit world.

"People think that masks are for hiding behind," the Owl said, "but truly, they are for being seen."

"Why do you have so many masks?" Pitu asked.

The Owl laughed a creeping chuckle. "Why, I wear them." The creature chuckled again. "And I trade them."

"Trade them?" Pitu asked. "With whom?"

"With shamans and spirits." The Owl answered plainly at first, then its voice changed, becoming more ominous. "Or with a wandering person, no magic within them."

"What does that mean?"

"That means," the Owl said, "that I will always help those who are angry enough to look for retribution."

A shiver slicked down Pitu's spine. Stories sprang in his memories, legends of mistreated people hurting those who had hurt them. Pitu had never seen any good in vengeance. It was a terrible way to look at life. A perpetuation of violence.

"An eye for an eye," the Owl said. "That's what I help those wanderers achieve."

Pitu scrunched his nose, "All you do is bring more pain to the people. How can you do that?"

The Owl chuckled once more, just as creepy and oily as before. "How do you think the spirits are born? How do you think we live on for centuries? Off kindness? No, no, no . . . we are born of pain. We are born of darkness. We are born to help those who suffer, just as we suffer."

Pitu remained silent. The Owl was not particularly threatening. Though Pitu felt uncomfortable with the idea that he was sitting in the cave with a spirit, talking of violent things, he also felt safe. The Owl did not seek the vengeance, only nurtured it. In the silence, the Owl looked back into the flames of the qulliq, waiting for a response from the shaman.

Never in his life would Pitu have thought that he'd be sitting next to an owl that took the shape of a person. A spirit that others thought was simply another shaman, using a mask to keep itself hidden. The people thought it was a mask meant to hide, but as the Owl had said, it wore the mask to be seen.

"And what about those of us who are not looking for retribution?" Pitu finally asked. "How do you help those of us who are more interested in helping than hurting?"

"Oh, I help them, too," the Owl answered sharply, annoyed. "But it's much less entertaining. The shaman comes, the shaman goes, the people stay away for many years . . . they always come back, though. It takes a while, but they always come back to me."

Again, a shiver swept through Pitu like a stream of water melted from ice slipping down his spine. He looked at the Owl. Into the slits in the mask that the Owl saw through. He said, "Will you help me go into the sea? Will you help me find my way to Nuliajuk?"

The Owl, who had seemed more mischievous than scary for the most part, suddenly changed in demeanour. The air in the cave seemed to shift back and forth between hazy and clear, making Pitu feel dizzy and nauseated. The Owl's shape grew fuzzy and elongated at one moment and shrunken the next. At once, the Owl was a grown man, a grown woman, an elder, a child. The flame of the qulliq dimmed and grew with the passing of each breath.

Pitu felt the pain of a budding headache as his eyes could not gauge what was happening. He stumbled backward, disoriented and for a moment feeling unsure and unsafe.

The Owl's voice boomed into the cave, "*You do not speak her name. You do not have that privilege.*"

Then, just as suddenly as the moment before, the qulliq flame stopped flashing and stabilized. As his eyesight adjusted back to normal, Pitu's headache ebbed but didn't quite go away. The Owl returned to the former shape it had taken.

"Ah, yes." The Owl ominously echoed the words it had spoken earlier. "*So young you are.*"

"I didn't mean to offend you," Pitu said quickly, "I'm sorr—"

"Of course, the young do not understand the ways of the ancient," the Owl interrupted. "And the arrogance of the young never fails to make an appearance. Your apologies have no meaning, and I will not accept them."

Fearful that he had jeopardized everything, Pitu used one of the oldest lessons he'd ever learned. The lesson of respecting those older than him—it held true for elders, and now for ancient spirits. He averted his eyes, remained silent, and waited to hear his admonishments.

The Owl was quiet for a moment, considering Pitu. When finally the Owl spoke, its voice was a mixture of dismissive and smug. "Ah, all that power given to you, all that worship and respect. The humans and the spirits have made you confident, and yet you are clumsy enough that you did not even know of such a basic rule."

Still, Pitu waited silently. He stared at the scraps of furs and bones on the floor.

"It is earned, yes, I know that," the Owl said, "that respect you've been given. It is. But you must maintain it. That's what they always seem to forget . . . once a shaman gains respect and recognition, they become lazy. They think they do not have to remain the thing that the spirits saw potential in."

Now, Pitu looked up. The Owl stared intensely at him, the expression on the mask seeming to have changed. The glittering behind the eyes no longer held mischief but something more vicious. The Owl's head tilted again, a gesture no longer only creepy, but also erratic and nasty. The Owl said, "You shamans, you go and do the bidding of us spirits. That is your purpose: to carry the life of the living and the spirits. Forever *I* will dwell in this cave, helping to right wrongs, helping women seek justice, helping forgotten spirits live again. Forever I nurse wounds that come from the terrible actions of others. Your purpose is to respect that and help to carry out what must be done."

A magnitude of questions occurred to Pitu, but he did not know which ones to ask. Why was the Owl the one Pitu had to seek out? Why was the Owl tasked with such a responsibility?

"Now," said the Owl, its voice and mask and eyes all changing once again. The mischief returned, the nonchalant and chuckling voice. "Ask your question again, but ask it the right way."

What the Owl had said had been true in some ways. Pitu had gone through much of his struggles and training with praise coming to him from many directions. The spirits revelled in his presence, his community was enthralled when he was close by; even the village they had just visited clung to his every word. He had always been told he was going in the right direction and hadn't been faced with many reprimands.

Well, that wasn't entirely true, he thought. There were times he had asked too many questions of Tagaaq, or had asked questions the wrong way. Tagaaq would reprimand him kindly, but lately Tagaaq was beginning to let his frustration show. Now Pitu could see the lesson he'd missed in those bursts of frustration. Pitu had simply assumed it was due to Tagaaq growing older and losing patience.

"So, what must I do?" Pitu asked. There was nothing more to ask, nothing more than what needed to be done. Pitu needed to learn how to survive beneath the ice and learn what he had to do to bring the animals back to the starving people. Hesitantly, he added, "How can I find . . . her?"

After an underwhelmed sigh, the Owl shrugged and said, "Well, I guess that's good enough."

The Owl stood up and walked around the cave, going through the masks. They were made from all sorts of materials. Some were dried animal hides, the fur scraped off, with white and black sinew used to mimic the patterns of tattoos on a woman's skin. Some masks used decorative feathers, some were still covered in fur. Some were even beaded with tiny shells. There was a particular pile of masks made from sealskin that were crafted in exquisite detail. The dark spots of the ringed seal fur stood out against the silver. Some masks covered one's whole face, while others only covered half. There were feminine masks, and masculine ones. There were small ones and large.

The Owl finally chose one—a plain sealskin mask with humble detail—and handed it to Pitu. "Put this on," the Owl said.

Still fearful from the Owl's earlier outburst, Pitu took the mask somehow with both haste and caution.

Pitu admired the sleek look of the sealskin. It would only cover the top half of his face, with holes cut out for his eyes to peer through. At the sides were strands of sinew string to tie the mask on, and a curve was cut into the bottom half of the mask to the shape of a nose. He tried it on, tying the string tightly around the back of his head. The inside of the mask was comfortable against his skin, the dried skins weathered and softened. It was like he was wearing a pair of sunglasses made from skin rather than bone.

The Owl tilted its head once more, stared at Pitu, then nodded in approval. The Owl said, "Shall we begin?"

12

Preparation

The Owl told Pitu to keep wearing the mask until it felt like a second skin. At first, Pitu felt comfortable wearing it. But now that he knew he was not allowed to remove it, the mask began to feel itchy, and he was too aware of its placement on his face. He could feel the tie at the back of his head and the clammy sweat that was caught between his skin and the mask.

"Have you ever heard stories of how other shamans would travel to her home under the sea?" the Owl asked.

Pitu thought of the shamans he had known in his life. There was Tagaaq's mother, Angugaattiaq, known to Pitu only through stories and a one-time encounter with her spirit. There was a man named Imiqqutailaq who had drum danced for the camp once when Pitu was a small boy. There was Taktuq, a revered shaman who had hidden himself in solitude when his power became too much to bear. Tagaaq had shared many stories about Angugaattiaq, but none had mentioned an encounter with Nuliajuk. Imiqqutailaq had only told the story of how he had become a shaman when he visited Pitu's camp. As for Taktuq, Pitu had heard that the old man had been to visit Nuliajuk, that he had combed her hair to release the animals, but he didn't know any other details. Taktuq had not been willing to share his past with Pitu, at least not without a certain amount of prodding.

"I have heard stories of shamans going to see her," Pitu answered. "But without mention of *how* they went there."

"All stories tell the same thing," the Owl said. "What do they do to appease her?"

"They comb her hair," Pitu replied.

The Owl nodded. "Do you have a comb to bring with you?"

Pitu scrunched his nose. His hair was long and tangled from being bunched up and stuffed into the hood of his parka. As a child, his mother had once brushed through his hair with a comb made from bone, but it kept getting caught in the knots. He had cried out in agony every time the comb had gotten caught and tore a strand or two from his scalp. Since then, he had refused to brush his hair.

"Then you must make one," the Owl said. The Owl went to a pile of bones on the floor of the cave and sifted through them, just as it had with the masks. When it found a smooth and thin shoulderblade from a seal, the Owl tossed it over to Pitu. "You cannot go to her with a comb you have borrowed. You have to give her your own, or a comb you have made especially for her. This shows how much you value her."

Pitu picked up the seal shoulderblade, but he didn't feel that he was much of a carver. He made his own tools, sure, but carving something that had to be decorative as well as purposeful was something he had never been able to do. Pitu also didn't have any carving equipment with him. The Owl waved a hand in the air. "_Poor little shaman,_" the Owl mocked. "I cannot give you the carving tools. It is only your tools that can craft the comb. Leave this cave. Return when your comb is complete. I am patient."

Pitu thanked the Owl, then slowly weaved his way out of the cave, looking down at the shoulderblade. Outside, the dogs had calmed enough to take their naps, and the men had made a comfortable camp, with an iglu large enough for them all to fit in together. Atiq was waiting, sitting on a qamutiik, a knife in one hand and a piece of caribou in the other. Tumma and Ka'lak must have been inside the iglu, dozing in the warmth of the burning seal fat in a qulliq. As Pitu made his way from the cave mouth to the camp, Atiq rose from the qamutiik, his arm outstretched with a piece of caribou for Pitu to eat. Pitu saw the fear on Atiq's face, and he remembered the sealskin mask that he was wearing.

"Thank you, little brother," Pitu said, without offering an explanation, "but I'm not hungry." He went straight to his hunting gear, packed onto the sled, and began looking for carving utensils.

The dogs remained motionless, but at the sound of his voice, Tumma emerged from the iglu. Pitu greeted his friend but did not volunteer to start a conversation. He was focused solely on crafting the comb. Finally, he found a slender piece of stone, smoothed by the making of blades and other hunting tools. Then he sat on the qamutiik and brought the stone to the shoulderblade. He began brushing and chiselling it against the bone.

"Why are you wearing that mask?" Tumma asked.

Pitu answered curtly, "It will help me in my journey."

A moment later, Tumma asked another question. "What are you making?"

"A comb," Pitu answered. He looked up at his oldest friend, seeing confusion on the faces of both Tumma and Atiq. He clarified, "A comb that I can use to brush Nuliajuk's hair."

At that, they both looked away. Pitu kept on carving, and they watched with fascination. Slowly, a shape began to emerge out of the bone. Perhaps it had been a few hours, perhaps longer, for the sun had long set. They sat outside as the day turned to evening and the cold crept deeper into their skin. The three of them began to shiver in the growing darkness. The moonlight was dim, but Pitu squinted as he continued his work.

Pitu's shoulders were sore from sitting hunched over. He stopped carving, looking up at his little brother and Tumma. He saw that they had fallen asleep on the ice as they watched him. Pitu's eyes danced with exhaustion, and he could see a calming blue light surrounding them all. It seemed that the spirits had come to watch Pitu's work, too.

Pitu's joints cracked as he stretched and yawned. He put the carving stone away, but he slipped the shoulderblade into his mitt for safekeeping. Tomorrow he would add the tines of the comb and decorate it with designs engraved into the handle. Then he would return to the cave and learn the next step in the journey.

He woke his brother and his friend. The three of them entered the iglu, where Ka'lak was already sleeping deeply. The three undressed, but Pitu kept on his mask. They all fell quickly asleep.

Again, Pitu dreamt of a day filled with sunlight shining down on him. Again, he felt the urge to store that sunlight, as animals store nutrients at the end of summer with the knowledge that winter brings darkness and little nourishment. He wanted to gather that sunlight, thinking that he would need it later, that it was important to keep.

Pitu was lying on a field of soft moss, Arctic cotton, bushes of berries and lichen. A herd of caribou, thousands of them, were grazing nearby. Closer still were dozens of hares and foxes, lemmings and ground squirrels, weasels and birds of all sorts, all living in harmony. The foxes were not stalking the animals. The lemmings and ground squirrels were not scurrying to hide in their burrows. All the creatures surrounding him were simply there, encouraging Pitu to store the light within.

It was at this moment, in this dream, that Pitu truly felt he understood the meaning of _peace_ among shamans. There had been moments in his life when he had felt peaceful, when he had felt the summer sunlight sinking into his flesh, bringing contentment and comfort with it. This moment brought another thought.

He thought of shamans who had abandoned their families and camps in search of peace. It was this feeling here and now that they sought, he realized. Pitu knew, however, that this feeling was not peace. No. It was power. The strength of thousands of spirits lending their thoughts and their wisdom and their hearts to him. This was not peace. This was the dangerous power that overwhelmed a shaman, that caused their souls to break under the pressure of power, drunk on this feeling.

Pitu looked around, more focused now. He searched for his tuurngaq among the foxes and spotted Tiri, flirting with the other foxes and animals. She, too, was persuaded by the power. Pitu always did what the spirits told him to do, but he made sure to stay critical. He could not simply accept this power. He had to respect it and take it in small doses.

Still, despite his skepticism, Pitu found a place to enjoy this feeling. He forgot about his heartbreak over Saima, his exasperation toward Qajaarjuaq, his concern for his mother, and his suspicion of the dark spirits at Aqiggiq's camp. Those were for his waking moments. Now, it was simply time to let his muscles relax and put his mind at ease. Life had more than enough things for him to worry over.

Pitu had been awake for hours, carving away at the bone, by the time any of the others got up. He had woken before the rise of the sun, his mask askew on his face. He fixed the mask, dressed, fed the dogs, and then took his seat on the qamutiik. Three long and thin teeth were now carved from the bone, looking fragile as Pitu worked on the last one.

Ka'lak emerged from the iglu, walking a small distance away to the area they had designated to relieve themselves. When he returned, the elder asked no questions and began no conversation. He ate a few pieces of meat, then went to work on his own crafts. Pitu enjoyed the elder's silent presence. It calmed him.

More time passed as the two of them worked alone, but together. Tumma was next to emerge, his eyes swollen with sleep. He, too, went off to the designated area to empty his bladder and bowels. When he returned, Tumma asked no questions, but followed the rhythm of Ka'lak and Pitu.

The three sat, working on their individual projects: Pitu the comb, Ka'lak a new harpoon head, and Tumma a new stone lamp. The morning passed in silent work.

At some point, Atiq emerged and followed the same routine as the three before him. He went to the designated spot. He returned for a few bites of meat, then sat in the snow with his toy bow in hand.

Without much thought, Pitu began to tell stories of his harrowing journey. Atiq knew the stories by heart, but Tumma was not as familiar with them, and Ka'lak had never heard them before. Pitu told them about the giant, and about the northern lights running across the sky. The others listened to the stories in silence.

When Pitu carved the last fragile tooth into the comb, he looked up to see that the three had stopped their crafting long before. They listened as Pitu told the final story—that of the black wolf urging Taktuq to kill Pitu, only to end up with Taktuq sacrificing himself to send Pitu back to the living world.

Now, Pitu held up the comb in the soothing sunlight. "The next story will be one where I dive into the sea and give Nuliajuk this comb," he said. Then more quietly, he added, "If I live."

Pitu went into the iglu and retrieved his qulliq, the flames long burned out. He wiped his finger through the soot residue and smudged it into the engravings he'd carved into the comb. The lines became stark against the sun-bleached bone.

The others wished Pitu luck before he began to make his way back to the cave. He weaved his way back through the tunnels, finding the Owl in the same spot as when he had left the day before. Pitu was sure that the Owl had not moved at all since.

The Owl, seeing Pitu enter, tilted its head in the same unsettling way as before. "Back so soon?"

Pitu held out the comb. "What now?"

A fish landed at Pitu's feet, a sculpin. "Eat the fish," the Owl advised.

Pitu hadn't realized how hungry he was. He hadn't eaten since the day before, prior to entering this cave. He knelt in front of the sculpin. He asked the Owl if there was a knife he could use to cut open the fish. The Owl handed Pitu a small ivory knife, and said, "Eat the whole fish. The guts, the spikes, the fins, the gills."

Though this was a strange request, Pitu did not question it. He devoured the sculpin. There was little meat on its body, but he relished every bite. Sculpins were casually known as "ugly fish." Pitu was surprised that most parts of the fish were not as unpleasant as he expected, and the spiky fins hurt on the way down his throat, but not terribly so. Pitu was able to stomach most of the fish's guts, but the Owl stopped him from eating parts that would make him sick. When he finished eating the fish, Pitu licked the fish oil from his fingers. He cleaned the small ivory knife, only slightly bigger than his middle finger, and offered it back to the Owl. The spirit waved it away, saying that it had no need for the knife. Without much thought, Pitu tucked the small knife into his mitt.

"How does the mask feel?" the Owl asked.

Pitu reached a hand up to touch the mask on his face. He'd forgotten he was still wearing it. The Owl chuckled. "It's remarkable how quick you are." The Owl stood. "Follow me, young shaman."

Pitu followed the Owl as he weaved his way through other tunnels in the cave. Eventually, they emerged on the other side of the lone mountain. The terrain looked almost exactly the same as where his friends were camping, except it was as though it were inverted. The hillsides were to the south rather than the north, the vast frozen ocean to the north rather than the south. The only other noticeable difference was a deep gash in the ice where his campsite would have been. The crack led to a polynya with a swelling current. A familiar sense enveloped Pitu, and anxiety swelled within him as the water swelled in the open sea.

He'd never been here in this particular place, but he knew where he was in a grand sense. Pitu felt a familiar churning in the air, a power that spread far and wide across the vast land. This was only a feeling, though, an inner sense. Around him there was almost an *absence* of weather; he saw no signs of life. He remembered that life was different in this place. It was not held to the same bounds as life was back home.

He had returned. He was back in the spirit world.

13

Ice

The Owl laughed again, sensing Pitu's discomfort. "Yes, our land remembers you. The spirits remember you," it crooned, sending sinister chills over Pitu's skin. "The qallupilluit remember you *very* well."

Pitu swallowed, pressure building in his throat, but there was no fighting the sickness he was feeling. Though Pitu had felt that he and the Owl had come to an understanding the day before, the creature was back to its eerie self. No longer showing anger outright, but still craving retribution, craving violence.

"Where do I go?" Pitu asked, staring out at the black water in the polynya. It did not look the least bit inviting.

"Leave your caribou parka in the mouth of the cave. Take off your caribou pants and boots," the Owl instructed.

Pitu looked back at the Owl, his cheeks growing red with embarrassment. "I have to go in *naked*?!"

The Owl tilted its head once more. "Of course not. Where are your clothes made from sealskin?"

Pitu thought of the sealskin parka, pants, and boots his mother had made for him, packed and tied up securely to his qamutiik on the other side of the mountain. He had a suspicion that he would not be allowed to retrieve them. He knew he would not be allowed to leave this world until his task was complete.

"They are tied up with my equipment on my qamutiik," Pitu said softly, embarrassed once again.

The Owl shook its head in amusement. "You thought you could venture beneath the ice in the skins of a land-ridden creature? Wait here." That horrible laugh again. Then the Owl mockingly added, "Don't let the spirits tempt you, *sweet little shaman*."

Pitu was certain that no spirit would ever tempt him out here, but as the Owl disappeared into the darkness of the cave, Pitu's confidence faltered. A sudden gust of wind blew in, and with it, voices echoed. They were voices he recognized—his mother's lilting songs, Saima's charming laugh, and even Ikuma's soft stories. He wanted to follow their voices.

In the span of a minute, the wind shifted once more, and the whole area changed. Clouds swarmed toward the mountain, falling into a misty fog. The current in the polynya quickened, and at its edge, a familiar creature appeared. A qallupilluq crawling out of the depths. Once on the ice, she stood, her hair falling in sickening tendrils.

All Pitu had was his comb and the small ivory knife the Owl had lent to him. Everything else he had left on his qamutiik. What would he do when she reached him? He was sure a qallupilluq wouldn't let him get away again. How foolish of him. He should have brought his beloved snow knife at least.

Suddenly, he noticed more figures coming through the thickening fog, along all the edges of the polynya and the thick crack in the ice. As soon as one was out of the water, another crawled out behind it.

Oh no. He had to run. Pitu had to run or they would kill him. But he was frozen, unsure of where to go. The qallupilluit were stalking closer and closer, surrounding him from all angles. Maybe Pitu would be able to go back into the cave? Would the qallupilluit follow him inside? Should he trust his instincts, or should he listen to the Owl's advice and stay exactly where he was?

The Owl returned a moment later, holding Pitu's clothing in its arms. The Owl handed the clothes over. Then without hesitation, the Owl stepped onto a path in the snow and ice. "*Avani,*" the Owl spoke in an assertive murmur. "Shoo. Go away."

The Owl waved its hands dismissively, *shooing* the qallupilluit back into the sea. Pitu was shocked as the qallupilluit fled from the Owl. All it did was simply wave them away, as a mother would drive her children away while she's busy sewing or looking after others, and they bolted.

The sky was beginning to clear again, the fog lifting. The Owl half-turned to look back at Pitu. "Go on," the Owl said. "Change into the sealskin."

The Owl continued to send the qallupilluit back into the water. Pitu changed as the Owl cleared the area, the sky still shifting back to overcast. When the qallupilluit were gone and the Owl had returned, Pitu couldn't help but say, "For someone who values revenge, you had no problem taking it away from the qallupilluit."

The Owl laughed. "The qallupilluit steal *children* and *babies*, Piturniq. They do not deserve their share of vengeance. I'm not a monster."

Pitu felt a great heaviness fall upon him as the Owl uttered his name for the first time. Up until now, the Owl had only been calling him "young shaman." He hadn't told the Owl his name, but it was no surprise that the Owl knew it. Bashfully, Pitu remembered using Nuliajuk's name with nonchalance. Now he truly understood the Owl's anger.

When a spirit used his name, Pitu always felt the great weight of responsibility mixed with incompetence sweep over him. How could he carry out tasks to save whole villages? How could he rival thousand-year-old spirits? If the Owl knew what using Pitu's name had meant, how it had made Pitu feel, the Owl showed no sign. Pitu felt that the Owl did know, and purposely used it to make Pitu feel that swell. The Owl had begun walking along the path again with its back to Pitu.

Pitu stayed back, lost in his thoughts. There were countless expectations that people placed on him,

and he didn't know if he could meet them all. After a moment, the Owl looked back at Pitu. Irritated, it said, "*Atii!* Come on!"

Pitu left his thoughts to stew, but he knew he would return to them sooner or later. He followed the path, worried that a qallupilluq might jump out from behind one of the large boulders in the area. Nothing happened.

The Owl stopped at the water's edge, by the wide crack in the ice. "Don't worry about the qallupilluit," it said. "Once you enter the water, you'll find your way. It will be known why you are there, and the qallupilluit do not touch anyone in the sea if they know you are going to see her."

"I can't swim," Pitu said. Heaviness was building within him, and the pressure in his throat led him to take quick, nervous breaths. "What do I do?"

Again, the Owl chuckled in disturbed delight. "She is waiting for you, Piturniq. Once you enter the water, you will know what to do. Trust the sea."

Pitu's fear grew, becoming more difficult to ignore and overcome. The edges of the crack looked sharp enough to pierce clean through his body, and he knew the water must be frigid. How could a mask and sealskin clothing be the only items needed to protect him from the ice and the vicious creatures beneath it?

Pitu hesitated. Why wouldn't the Owl just tell him what was going to happen? At least then Pitu would feel more at ease. Possibly. A sneaking thought entered his mind: *I don't think I'll ever feel at ease again.*

Suddenly Pitu felt hands dig into his arms, sharp nails piercing through his parka and deep into his skin. Pitu tried to throw the hands off, but as he looked around, he saw that it was the Owl digging its claws into him. The mask looked as if it were smiling.

"Good luck, young shaman," the Owl hooted, as it pushed Pitu into the depths.

The water was glacial, crushing the breath out of his lungs and squeezing his stomach tight. His thoughts and worries left his mind, and all that remained was panic rushing through his entire body. As he sank beneath the ice, Pitu felt as though he was being stabbed from all directions. For a moment, he thought it might be the qallupilluit, their long, sharp nails piercing through him. Eventually, Pitu opened his eyes, and for a moment they burned, but he could see that he was alone in the darkness. Soon the burn dissipated. He looked around, and above him he could see a jagged cast of light. It shrank as he sank lower and lower. As he descended, as he watched that light drifting farther and blurring with the salt and ice, a calmness engulfed him.

Pitu held his breath, but he also felt the absence of needing to breathe. His arms and legs were open wide, and the current kept pulling him deeper into the ocean. The stabbing pain of the cold had stopped, and now Pitu only felt numb. The light had disappeared completely now. Though he was surrounded by darkness, Pitu was comfortable in it.

His eyes began to adjust in the darkness, and suddenly there was no darkness at all. The water surrounding him had turned a beautiful shade of blue, and inexplicable floes of ice floated around him. The floes cast bright lights that were unlike either sunlight or moonlight. Their soft glow created an exquisite colourful aura.

This isn't how nature works, Pitu thought. He revelled in the beauty and power this place had. It was terrible and unnatural, but it was breathtaking, overwhelming, and humbling. This was not the remarkable awe of *life*, it was the remarkable awe of *after* and *before* and *forever*, all at once. He savoured the feeling, as he had the night before in his dream of all those animals, and he remembered that this was a privilege.

His back landed on the floor of the sea. Sand, ice, and seaweed drifted in the flow. There was nothing else around, no sign of Nuliajuk, no sign of animals, and no sign of creatures of any sort. He was thankful for that last fact. He sat up, his motions feeling slow and delayed. His hair drifted upward. Slowly, Pitu stood. He expected to float, but it was as if rocks were weighing down his clothing. He took his first steps on the ocean floor.

The walk was long and slow. He saw nothing but the floes of ice and the floating seaweed. The farther he went, the more things began to appear— large boulders, strange plants, and sea mollusks. Still, there were no signs of any larger animals or mammals.

It took a long time to go wherever he had to go. He wasn't sure where he was being led, but the pull of the current was taking him forward, and the farther he walked, the more beautiful and peculiar the path appeared. Not a single breath escaped his lungs. Not a single patch of skin froze in the frigid water. After a while, he couldn't tell if he was awake or if he was dreaming. Before his eyes, boulders turned into whale bones. Ice floes looked more like the abandoned remains of igluit made from ice. And stacked stone inuksuit littered the bottom of the sea.

He stopped for a moment. Darkness had returned—black as soot—and ash fell in inky sweeps around him. There was nothing here. Perhaps Nuliajuk had once been here, surrounded by her animals, but now all that was left were ancient ruins. Had she moved on? Had this trip been a hopeless task from the beginning? There was no meaning in being here. Nuliajuk had abandoned this place, just as she had abandoned the starving village. Pitu lost hope . . .

Then, suddenly, he stumbled over a mound of ice. Just as suddenly, a seal swam quickly past him and then disappeared.

"Ah, so the boy has arrived," said a powerful voice.

And she appeared. Nuliajuk. The spirit of the sea and the mother of sea mammals.

14

The Woman Below

Her presence was incomprehensible.

Long, long, long black hair flowed behind and all around her. At first, Pitu had thought the darkness was due to the depth of the ocean, but now he could see and feel that it was her hair. Strands the length of bowhead whales upon bowhead whales. Fish, seals, even a narwhal were tangled into the length of it, while other animals swam to the depths and passed breaths of bubbles toward the tangled creatures so they wouldn't drown. Though Nuliajuk's hair was massive and full of tangled animals, it remained beautiful and elegant.

Beneath her hair, Nuliajuk had a face of extraordinary beauty. Memories of stories about her sprang to Pitu's mind—how she'd had many suitors proposing marriage to her when she had been human.

Graceful tattoos were inked into her skin; extravagant v-shapes were outlined in the centre of her forehead, with dots in between the lines. Across her cheeks were similar shapes, but the dots were inside, lining up across her cheekbones. From her lower lip to her chin and jaw there were lines, and every second line was dashed. Even across her collarbone, beneath her amauti, Pitu could see tattoos. The tattoos oozed her wisdom and power, her greatness.

She herself was no larger than Pitu. For some reason, he had thought she would be the size of the whales that were her children, and he had also expected her to have an appearance similar to the qallupilluit. Still, despite her height, she was anything but average. She looked regal and strong. Her amauti was covered in the most beautiful sealskin designs and was decorated with seashells.

Beneath her amauti, Nuliajuk had no legs. Instead she had the tail of a fish, covered in beautiful, iridescent scales of a light yellowish-green hue. She floated slightly off the ocean floor. A sense within the water told Pitu that her tail was a sign that although she was the mother of all sea mammals, she was also a part of the sea. She commanded fish and mollusks and seaweed. The ocean, in its reverence and love for her, gifted the fish tail to her in acceptance and appreciation of her power.

Pitu did not know what to do. Should he bow? Should he kneel and kiss her . . . tail?

"Oh, young shaman." Nuliajuk chuckled lightly. Her voice was soft, yet still formidable and powerful. "I can feel you shaking from here."

She spoke with the same humour the Owl spoke with—teasing, with a disconcerting manner. She was still quite a length away, slightly shrouded by the murkiness of the ocean. Pitu dared not go closer, afraid that approaching might be disrespectful.

"You are the one that the spirits have been telling me about," Nuliajuk continued. The words oozed gracefully from her lips. "The shaman of light?"

"If that is what they call me," Pitu affirmed, still unsure what to do. His voice sounded thin and incredibly human.

Nuliajuk swiftly swam forward, rushing toward Pitu. Her nose touched his for a moment before she pulled herself back. He'd hardly seen her movement. Now he could see her fully. He was awed. Her skin had paled from the lack of sunlight, but she was as radiant as the full moon. Pitu caught sight of her hands, and he could see that she had no fingers. Instead, her hands stopped at the ends of her knuckles. More tattoos covered her hands, depicting the symbols of the qulliq flames, the mountains, and fertility.

She tilted her head, the exact same way the Owl had. Though the Owl had worn a mask, Pitu couldn't help but see them in each other. The mannerisms and overall presence of both were overwhelming. She spoke once more, her tone accusing. "You've come from the dark village."

"Yes," Pitu said, the words barely coming out as she invited him to speak. "They are dying, and they have no strength to move to a new place."

"The spirits there are dark, young shaman." Nuliajuk's face darkened, her eyes narrowing. "When my animals return from that place, they bring the shadows with them. I am _sick_ of shadows."

Her voice had changed. As her expression darkened, her voice deepened, her previous tenor overlapping with something much deeper and perhaps angered. Pitu wished he could move away from her, but he couldn't gauge how she would interpret it. Their noses were still only a small movement away from touching. He couldn't decide if stepping away would be seen as disrespectful, or if not stepping away would be seen as aggressive. He stayed still, paralyzed by indecision.

"However, young shaman," Nuliajuk continued, her voice turning playful and mischievous, "you've come from the shadows, but they do not touch you. You are made of light. How can this be? You have seen darkness. I know your story with the dark wolf. I know you have killed qallupilluit and you have seen your friend die. How can it be that you are still as bright as the sun? The sun that I have not seen for centuries." Her expression had changed yet again, her eyes still narrow, but her mouth turned up into a smile.

Pitu was shaking. He had no answer. The face she was making, though it could have seemed friendly, made him uncomfortable.

Nuliajuk swam backward, opening the space in front of him. Her hair surrounded them, and her sudden movement caused it to move into a bubbled shape, similar to an iglu. Pitu imagined the hair closing in around him, blacking out the light, suffocating him. He didn't speak, and Nuliajuk's mischievous smile deepened. Sounding slightly surprised, she said, "Ah, a shy shaman. How refreshing."

"Not shy," Pitu said, not knowing why he was speaking. "I do not know why I have not been tempted by the shadows."

He thought of his dreams. The sunlight shining down, the animals there to praise and encourage him. *Do other shamans have those dreams?*

She narrowed her eyes. The smile on her face twisted as she said, "I do not trust the darkness you left. I do not trust that it hasn't touched you."

Pitu thought of the village. He had felt uncomfortable there. He had felt the spirits, but he couldn't reach them. Now, he wondered if the spirits had been able to reach him. Had they found a way to cling to him? He wasn't sure, but he was tired of people assuming he was susceptible to darkness. He'd proven many times that it was light he bore. Pitu spoke with growing confidence. "I trust that it hasn't. Too often people are unsure of whether I will fall to dark spirits, but I only want to help."

Nuliajuk had a skeptical look on her face, but he could see that she was considering what he said carefully. For a moment they shared no words, both deep in thought, staring at one another. Pitu felt the comb in his mitt, and he was reminded of the task he would have to complete to free the animals. He stared at her hair. The strands stetched out longer than he could see, and they were full of animals. It could take a lifetime to comb her hair.

A thought occurred to Pitu. She had said that

she took the animals away from the community because she was sick of the shadows they brought back. She didn't trust the spirits. He had thought it was Nuliajuk who had sent the dark spirits there in the first place.

"Were you not the one to send the spirits to the village?" he asked.

Nuliajuk's expression changed, her voice shifting from skeptical to offended. "I have nothing to do with dark spirits. What are you accusing me of?"

Pitu put up his mitts, palms facing her in submission. He scrunched his nose. "I apologize for my mistake. I did not know where the spirits were from, or how they got there. I assumed that you took the animals away and sent the spirits in their place."

"Do you think so little of me?" Nuliajuk snapped, her face changing once again. Shadows grew in the hollows of her face, a sneer making the structure of her bones look sinister. "Taking animals away is enough of a punishment. It was a person of that village—a wronged person—who brought the spirits there. I did not take my sea creatures away out of spite. I did it out of self-preservation."

This shocked Pitu. He thought of the village. He had liked the people he had met. They had been good and welcoming. He had been intimidated by Aqiggiq, but he trusted she was only trying to do what was best for her people. Pitu's thoughts sorted through all those he had met there, knowing that one of them had fooled him.

He thought of Ikuma, and almost instantly, he knew it was her. She was a mistreated orphan. Of the people he had met, she was the only one who fit the idea of a wronged person. Though perhaps he could also consider Ikuma's grandmother, he knew that she had grown too weak to call the dark spirits. Even if she had used the last of her strength to do so, she would have died, or he would have felt it when he'd relieved her pain during his visit. Now, he could see Ikuma's own strength, her ability to shroud this darkness in her own sorrow. His heart ached, for in the short time he had known her, she had become someone special, someone he could see easing his longing for Saima.

What would it mean now that he knew she was the one who brought the darkness?

"I can get rid of the spirits there. I know I can," Pitu said. Now that he knew, it became clear what he had to do. "Will you send the animals back once I rid them?"

"If they are gone, the animals will roam wherever they please," Nuliajuk answered, nonchalant and yet firm all at once. "The confidence of a shaman is nothing until his power is proven."

Pitu took the comb out of his mitt. It was delicate, barely as big as his palm. He showed it to Nuliajuk, her tendrils of hair reaching around them both and far beyond. She gave him the barest smile, and for once it didn't frighten him. Her smile was genuine as she admired the comb. She swam closer to him, her fingerless hands reaching out to touch it. "This is beautiful," she said.

In their closeness, Pitu could see more than a beautiful and frightening woman at the bottom of the ocean. Her hands, void of fingers, almost seemed to have no purpose. Yet there they were, soft and elegant, as she reached out to stroke the comb. She did not touch his skin, but her hand rested on the comb. His eyes moved from her hands to her face. She was pale, having had no contact with the sky and sun for millennia. She looked young, not much older than him.

It was no wonder the stories said she was vengeful. It was no wonder she responded to a single slight in anger. She had been nothing more than a young woman when her father had led her to her death.

"All who come here must comb and braid my hair, young shaman," Nuliajuk said. She moved her eyes from the comb and looked at Pitu for a moment. She raised her hands to his face, wriggling the knuckles of her absent fingers. "My hands are useless."

Pitu raised his eyebrows. "I made this comb for you." He let her hold it for a moment. They both stared at the piece of bone, admiring the craftsmanship Pitu had put into it. There was a rounded handle at one end, then it dipped inward and back out, widening to the carved tines. On both sides of the thin yet durable comb were etchings, lined and dotted, almost matching her tattoos. The leftover soot from the qulliq Pitu had dipped into the engravings made the intricate designs stand out more. "I would like to brush your hair now, and then it will be yours," he said after they had been staring at it for a while.

Nuliajuk handed it back to Pitu. "I hope that I will have it for a long time. The animals like to steal my nice things." She arched an eyebrow conspiratorially, looking at the animals that had begun to gather around them.

Pitu smiled, surprised by her quick change in nature. She flitted from emotion to emotion so quickly that Pitu felt his reactions could not keep up. He put his mitts into his sleeves and brought the comb to her hair.

"Silly young shaman," Nuliajuk said, her tone both playful and condescending. "To comb one's hair, you must begin from the very end and make your way upward to the root."

Pitu raised his brows in understanding, and he walked his way to the ends of her hair. It took him several moments to reach the floating ends, and when he looked back Nuliajuk was shrouded in the black strands of her hair. He began combing, but the overwhelming length and thickness of her hair was no match for the tiny comb he had crafted. He wondered if the Owl knew her hair was so long and unruly. Had the Owl knowingly sent Pitu to the bottom of the sea with a comb that hardly untangled a handful of Nuliajuk's hair?

He could have cursed the Owl, but instead he laughed.

Nuliajuk turned her head, peering at the laughing boy. Her brow was arched yet again, though she did not appear angry. Pitu stopped his laughter. He called out, "I have only ever brushed my younger sister's hair once or twice. This will take many days for me to comb."

"A shaman must do what he has to," Nuliajuk replied dismissively, finding entertainment in the seals chasing fishes in front of her.

So, Pitu did what he had to. Untangling every knot, releasing every fish or mammal stuck in her hair. He found other things, too—seaweed and coral, critters like urchins and mussels. He released them all until he reached her scalp.

"Ah," Nuliajuk said as he showed her the beautifully flowing loose strands. "There is one lock of hair complete."

His back ached. His fingers had gone numb a long time ago. He still had the rest of her hair to detangle. Then he would have to braid it all. Pitu began his walk back to the ends of her hair.

"You are a determined young shaman," Nuliajuk murmured, her voice trailing behind him. "Usually the others take a rest now. They spend days and days with me as they work through the tangles."

Pitu thought of resting, of lying down at the bottom of the sea. A sea full of bottom-dwelling ice floes, sea monsters, and a lone spirit. What was it like to live here, alone but for animals as company? Nuliajuk may have been frightening and unreadable, but Pitu knew one thing—if one drew breath in the world, then one knew of loneliness.

"Would you like me to rest?" Pitu asked her. His shoulders ached enough that he wouldn't mind the break.

She dismissed his question. "Though you are the first to ask, I do not really care. I can see your longing to return to your people. It is not often I am visited by such an inexperienced shaman, one who is still so full of desire to help others. It is quite interesting to see such determination."

With that, he continued his combing, finding more and more animals and plants in her hair. Clams, moss, and jellyfish. He tossed each of them aside to swim away as he freed them from her hair, moving up and up, on and on.

At one point, frustrated with a particularly difficult knot, Pitu left the strands he was working on. He swam toward the larger creatures tangled in the hair, a walrus and a narwhal. They thrashed as he closed in, their tusks rocking as they tried to reach him. Pitu remained calm as he worked to let them free of the hair. As soon as they could wriggle free, they swam toward the surface, disappearing into the murk.

He returned to the knot he had been working on previously, only to realize he had lost it. He would have to start all over again.

Instead of frustration, Pitu felt defeat. He grabbed a new handful of hair, followed its length until he reached the ends. He began the process of combing anew.

Hours passed. The ache in his shoulders spread to the whole of his body, and his lower back throbbed in tired pain. His elbows were sore, and his fingers felt raw from the repetitive motion of combing through knots and tangles. His throat grew thirsty in his exhaustion. Pitu, once again, lost grip of her hair and dropped the comb. He reached to grab them both, but in his dazed fatigue, the hair he had been working on blended in with the strands around him and he lost all his progress.

"Forgive me," Pitu suddenly sighed, "but may I ask you a foolish question?"

Nuliajuk raised her eyebrows and sardonically replied, "Those are my favourite kinds of questions."

"Please don't be offended, but I want to ask." Pitu looked toward her incredible length of hair and thought about how he kept losing any progress he'd made in combing it. With a deep, shaky breath, he asked, "May I cut your hair?"

She blinked at him for a moment, her mouth tightly pursed. He regretted the question as soon as he had asked it. The ache of his muscles had become too deep, reaching into his mind to cloud his thoughts. He had said those words before he could think.

Nuliajuk turned her head, looking at the length of hair flowing behind her. Silently, she looked back and forth between Pitu and her hair. Finally, she looked at Pitu fully. "I've lived here for millennia. I've been visited by countless men. My hair has been combed for eternity. Not once has a man offered such a ridiculous idea. A shortcut through the task!"

Pitu lowered his gaze. "I'm sorry," he said pitifully.

"Do not interrupt me," she snapped. "Did you think I was finished?"

Pitu did not speak. He did not make a single sound or movement.

"For millennia," Nuliajuk began again, "I've been visited by time-wasters." Pitu looked up suddenly. "I've been visited by men who are slimier than fish. Men who foolishly attempt to take advantage of me. Men who only breathe through their ugly mouths. Men who think they are deities themselves. Yet here you are, trying to take a shortcut."

Confusion swarmed through Pitu. He couldn't tell if she was scolding him or praising him. He waited for her to finish.

"My hair means little to me," Nuliajuk said, her voice calming. "It shrouds me in yet more darkness. I have already told you that I am sick of shadows." She looked at him, not smiling, but with amusement glittering in her eyes. "Again, your determination inspires me."

He remained still and quiet. Waiting.

"Yes," Nuliajuk spoke. "You may cut my hair. You will still have to comb and braid it, but cutting it will help us both."

Pitu still had the ivory knife that the Owl had lent him to eat the sculpin. He took it out now, removing it from his mitt and showing it to Nuliajuk. She gazed at it for only a moment. Then she told him, "Only one other shaman has offered to cut my hair before you."

He looked at her in confusion. Only a moment ago she had said no other man had thought to offer cutting her hair. She stared at the knife, at its fine build. "That knife belonged to her," Nuliajuk continued. "How did you get it?"

Pitu looked at the knife. The Owl must have known that Pitu would think of cutting her hair. He shrugged. "It was given to me."

"She had skin darkened by sunlight, in the heat of summer," Nuliajuk recounted. "Her amauti was beautiful and unique, and her hair was braided into intricate plaits."

Familiarity enveloped Pitu's memory as he remembered the spirit who had entered the qaggiq all those weeks ago. She had stormed in, reprimanding Pitu for wasting Nuliajuk's time with stories and celebration.

"Yes," Pitu said. "I have seen her before."

"She came here with her knife," Nuliajuk said. "This knife. No comb, no offering except to cut my hair and tie it up with nothing more than a piece of sinew. She knew the troubles of long hair."

He said nothing, only nodded.

"Since then, it has only been men," Nuliajuk whispered, annoyed and exhausted. "Men who do not know a woman's hair. Men who think that I want only to look beautiful."

She was lost in her memories now, spiralling down to the thoughts of those shamans. Pitu wondered why none of them had thought of cutting her hair. He had always thought that efficiency was one of the driving forces of humankind. He had always valued finding a way to make a task easier and taking advantage of one's circumstances. Perhaps the men had been too taken aback by Nuliajuk, unable to think outside of what they had always been told or known.

"Atii," Nuliajuk said. "Cut it."

Pitu began gathering a handful of her hair into his fist. He took a deep breath. Then—almost effortlessly—he sliced through the lock of hair.

In front of his eyes, the strands of cut hair gathered and began to move. They jutted to and fro for a moment before taking shape upon shape upon shape. Ugly fish, spiky and fat, swam around him.

Nuliajuk cooed softly, "*Kanajuit*. Sculpins."

They swam slowly, sliding past Pitu and toward Nuliajuk. She caressed them all for a moment, then the shoal of fish swam away. Pitu and Nuliajuk watched them go, disappearing into the dark depths.

Pitu said nothing. He didn't know what to say. He was sure that his jaw was still hanging wide open, his eyes unblinking.

"Piturniq," Nuliajuk said, and again Pitu felt that deep sense of heaviness, the incompetence and responsibility of his role as she used his name for the first time. Except this time, another feeling swept over him as well. *Power.* "The spirits have many names for you, and now you are given yet another. Kanajuq, sculpin, ugly fish. You will always be bound to the ocean."

"I don't understand," he said, his voice hoarse. The words were second nature to him, his response to almost every new thing he learned.

She laughed. "You have been so afraid of the sea, so afraid of the creatures here, but you were always meant to come here, to see me."

"What does that mean?" Pitu asked, terror shooting through him. "Will I ever go back up to the land?"

"Hah!" She let out another short-tempered laugh and waved her hand. "Yes, of course. Perhaps in another life you will be one of my sculpins, bound to me until you are eaten by the next visiting shaman. For now, you are still bound to that fox you call Tiri."

Pitu remembered a feeling he had had last summer, when he was in his qajaq on the foggy ocean. He had felt a great calm, a great sense of belonging. He could feel the fish and the seals beneath him just as he could feel the wiggle of his toes. He'd thought it was peace. Now . . . it became as clear as freshwater ice. It was his connection to the sea. *Forever bound to it.*

They were quiet, again, for a long period of time. Naturally, Pitu went back to her hair, continuing to grab handfuls and cutting it as evenly as he could. Each time he cut the hair free, the same transformation happened. Once he was done cutting, he wrapped the knife back into his mitt. He went back to comb the remains of her hair, and he braided it as he had braided Arnaapik's once before. It was loose, but he bound it with a strand of sinew he had cut from the laces of his kamiik.

Nuliajuk reached back, touching the silky and shiny braid. She shrugged. "It's loose, but that's probably as good as you can do. When you return to your life and family, you should practise. If you ever visit me again, I won't be so easy on you."

Pitu smiled tightly, thinking of Anaana and Arnaapik. Perhaps Anaana would let him braid her hair, but he was sure Arnaapik was at her wit's end with dealing with her brothers. She was at the age where women are truly terrifying—teenage womanhood.

"You are free to leave," Nuliajuk said, interrupting his thoughts. "Before you go, however, I do have some things I must share."

He waited in silence.

The expression on her face was a mixture of the mischief he'd grown used to and something that resembled authoritative discipline. Her youthful look changed once again—this time she became utterly ethereal and regal.

"You may be a part of this ocean now," she said, the mix of other tenors coming back into her voice, "but you are still subject to life and its boundaries. Its rules. You mustn't roam after your forbidden wants. You mustn't disrespect what has been put in place and what has been set in motion." She waved her fingerless hands, then continued, "You've been careless in the company you've been keeping. You've held onto the idea that you are still entitled to make mistakes. That is no longer the case. You, as a shaman, must follow the boundaries to the utmost degree. You must heed each and every single warning. Your charm has saved you thus far, but it will not last. The qallupilluit are angry. They may be vile creatures, but they do have a purpose, to take children from negligent parents as punishment. Dark spirits know of you because of what you did to their companions. Be careful. You may be connected to the ocean's spirit, but our creatures do not welcome newcomers so easily."

He remained silent.

"Remember, the animals are free to roam," she went on, "but they will not go to the dark village until the spirits are gone. You've proven to be clever, but you still have to prove your strength."

Agreeing, he raised his eyebrows. Pitu reached his hand out to offer the comb to her. She tilted her head in questioning, but then she gestured her hands toward her head. He placed the comb in her hair, an accessory for a woman of great fortitude.

He was half turned away when she said, "Kanajuq?"

He turned back. "The girl you love . . ." Nuliajuk continued, ". . . the one who is already bound to another. . . . You must leave the thought that you may have her someday. It is sad that you did not end up together, but life must carry on. Love changes. It always does. Holding onto a broken love, hoping it doesn't change, only leads to pain."

"Do you think I am the only one holding on?" Pitu asked. "I think she is clinging just as much as I am."

"What you say is true," Nuliajuk replied. She was slowly fading into the darkness, swimming away from him. "But remember that clinging too tightly bruises."

Then she was gone. Just as suddenly as she had appeared, she vanished.

15

Nagliktaujuq

Pitu began to swim, not quite sure if he was doing it right. Somehow, he was moving upward, though he felt in some way that he was floundering. He supposed it was another gift from Nuliajuk, a current to help him rise.

He passed the glowing ice floes, and as he kept rising, he saw more life in the sea than he had when he'd been sinking. Seals swam swiftly, narwhals rose and fell in lazy sweeps, fish darted from their hiding spots among the rocks.

The crack in the ice he'd been pushed into grew larger as he approached, the bright sunlight of the surface almost blinding him. The water was clear enough that Pitu could see Tiri up there, her eyes boring straight into his. A moment later, she began to fidget, pacing back and forth. *Watch out!*

Too late. Pitu realized he was no longer surrounded by lively swimming animals. Out of the corner of his eye, he could see a woman next to him. He turned toward her, wondering why Nuliajuk had ventured this high. Yet, as he saw the woman, he was struck by a different, yet still familiar, face. It felt unpleasant and haunting. Hollow cheeks, mottled grey skin stretched taut over harsh bones. Long, sharp nails were already reaching toward him, and Pitu couldn't avoid the scratching nail that was already digging into his skin. He tried to move away, but he could see that a throng of qallupilluit surrounded him.

They took hold of him, taking him from the current and pulling him under the thick ice, away from the crack, away from the surface.

Outside of the current, Pitu couldn't breathe. Suddenly the power of the ocean was strangling him—

the freezing cold, the ice and salt stabbing him. The qallupilluit simply watched as Pitu began to drown. Moments ago, Nuliajuk had told him that he was bound to the ocean, but now the ocean wanted nothing more than to suffocate him.

His vision went in and out of blackness. The grinning faces of the qallupilluit, sharp and ugly, burned into his eyes with the salt. He stopped struggling against the water, hoping beyond hope that he'd somehow save enough energy to survive.

In one moment, he saw the qallupilluit. In another, blackness.

Qallupilluit. Black. Qallupilluit. Black. Black. Black. Black. Black. Black. Black.

Once more, he came out of unconsciousness. He saw no qallupilluit. Another second of black. . . . Then . . .

A school of ugly fish.

Then black. Black. Black. Black. Black.

He could hear a girl crying.

Deep, guttural sobs that left one's throat raw and one's eyes burning. It was too dark to see.

Pitu tried to call out, to tell the girl that she wasn't alone, but his lungs were full of water. He couldn't move.

Her cries were excruciating. The kind that made a person hearing them cry just from the sound of them. She screamed into the nothingness. It wasn't a cry of physical pain. It was a cry of terror and utter disbelief.

It was pure anguish, rattling bones and hearts. Pain, not physical, but emotional.

He wanted to help her. He wanted to help her.

But Pitu couldn't move. He couldn't breathe.

The black was fading, and Pitu felt air in his lungs. Through his eyelids, he could see brightness, and on his skin, he could feel wind.

It took a great deal of effort to open his heavy eyes. Just opening them a sliver blinded him. He shut his eyes tightly. Even then, the squeezing of his eyelids was painful.

He lay there, taking short breaths as his lungs remembered how to inhale and exhale. He had no idea where he was, but he wasn't in the water anymore. Maybe the Owl had found and saved him.

His body took its time adjusting to the new place. Pitu could still taste salt water all over his mouth. He felt his bare hands on the rough surface of the ice. He must have lost his mitts in the . . . in whatever had happened. His ears were sloshing with water, but he could hear muffled sounds. His eyes slowly opened. Through his lashes he could see a clear blue sky. On the air, he smelled wet sealskin.

When his eyes were used to the light, he opened them wider, but still he could only see the sky.

There wasn't a bit of strength in his body to move. He would have to wait a while to be able to sit up and take in more. For now, he rested. His eyes darted back and forth, staring up at the bright sky. No clouds in sight, no birds flying overhead.

A moment later, a fox appeared. Her coat was vibrantly white with wafts of colourful smoke blurring her edges. She sniffed at his face, then licked his cheeks. Pitu's throat was too raw to greet her and tell her to stop licking him.

The sculpins saved you. Her voice was interlaced with concern and jealousy. *Where did they come from? Why do they feel like they are connected to you?*

Pitu struggled to speak. He coughed, pain filling his abdomen. He croaked, "Where are we?"

She didn't answer, instead urging Pitu to sit up. Her nose nudged against his head while she yipped into his ears, making them ring. Annoyed, Pitu mustered all his strength to push himself up so he could finally see what surrounded him. He was on a snow-covered seashore, his feet on the edge of an open crevasse in the ice. Further from the beach, on shoreline foothills, were other people.

Only they weren't *people*. He could see them huddling for warmth, paying no attention to him. Their parkas were all faded white, blending in with the snow. If it hadn't been a blue day, they'd have been almost invisible against a clouded sky. A vague memory sprang into his mind, a story that Tagaaq had once told him.

They were all spirits, dozens of souls with erased faces.

His exhaustion lessened. Pitu stood up, ignoring the ache in his bones and skin and muscles. Tiri urged him back to the water, to leave this place, but Pitu paid her no mind. Slowly, he made his way toward the faceless spirits. Not afraid, but full of the surety that he could help them. Tiri followed closely, staying by Pitu's feet.

He reached a spirit. It was a little farther from the others, closer to where Pitu had been. Again, Tiri urged him not to get any closer, but he continued to ignore her warning. Pitu touched the spirit's shoulder, and with that touch, its facial features bloomed. First, dark brown eyes and inquisitive eyebrows appeared, then the rest of a face—high cheekbones, tattooed forehead, and full lips. The woman looked at him, resentment twisting her face. Tiri reprimanded him, *Unaruluk! Look what you've done!*

But still, Pitu knew that he must help these spirits, that he had something to offer them. He disregarded Tiri once more and asked the woman, "Who are you?"

The woman looked away, taking in her surroundings. She saw the others, their pale blankness. A mist seemed to hang over all of them. Her eyes returned to Pitu and she said, "I don't know."

Tiri seemed to give up the fight, defeated. The spirit of the woman appeared to crumple in misery. Her eyes watered, and she squeezed them tightly shut. Pitu thought about reaching out to wrap an arm around her, but it didn't seem like the right thing to do. He stayed with her while she cried quietly. Grief was pouring out of her. He stayed quiet, not wanting to make her feel as though she needed to explain anything to him.

She whispered, "I only remember *him*. . . . His big hands hurting me over and over again. I remember not being able to breathe."

Pitu felt chills go down his spine, his stomach turning.

"Someone came and stopped him from hurting me—then I ran away. . . . I ran until my legs couldn't move anymore. I went to sleep. . . ." She was quiet for a moment, her brows furrowed in thought as she remembered and told him the details. "I—I woke up here, but there were more—there were more of us here." She looked back at the other spirits. "They used to be awake . . . but then our guardians . . . they left us and we—we began to fade."

"Who were your guardians?" Pitu asked her, but privately he thought, *What were the guardians?*

"Caregivers," she said. "They made us feel loved. They helped us heal our pain."

In Tagaaq's story, there was a place in the spirit world that belonged to Naglitaujuit, the souls of neglected and abused people. They came here to feel welcomed, accepted, and loved. Yet, they had been left to fade away with the same neglect that brought them here in the first place.

He wondered what had happened to the caregivers, why they had left these spirits that so deserved a better life. Pitu remembered the girl he had heard crying when he was stuck in unconsciousness and how much he had wanted to go and help her.

"They left to help someone," Pitu said, "didn't they?"

The spirit cried more, this time coming closer to Pitu and falling into his embrace. Her hands gripped the front of his parka and she sobbed into his chest. "They left us," she cried. "They left us, just as everyone leaves us."

He held her for a long time, patting her back. Again, Tiri whispered, *We must leave this place. You are unsafe. I could lose you.*

But Pitu couldn't leave this woman alone and crying. He whispered back, "We can stay a little longer."

We cannot stay! Tiri continued to nag. She spoke forcefully. *If you stay, you will never leave!*

Finally, Pitu realized what she was saying. He remembered a part of Tagaaq's story, though it had been such a minute detail that he had thought it might not be important. In the story, Tagaaq's mother had been in the shape of a bird, knowing that as a person, her spirit would be claimed.

Pitu pried the girl from his chest, peeling her strong grip from the sealskin. He said to her, "Let's wake some others. You can take care of each other."

This also upset Tiri. *No! We must leave. The more you wake, the more difficult it will be!*

"I can't just leave her here alone," Pitu said. "I have to help them."

Tiri whined, angry and frustrated. She followed him into the field of spirits, biting at his heels as her yips became more earnest.

Pitu and the woman walked to the other spirits, waking several others with a soft touch to their shoulders or chests. As more woke, more crying ensued. Heartbroken moans engulfed the snow-covered shoreline and sea ice.

Very quickly, Pitu realized that he should have listened to Tiri. The place had persuaded him to help, and his need to help clouded him from listening to his tuurngaq. Now, he was surrounded by spirits haunted by abuse and pain. He remembered now that even though the Naglitajuit were taken care of here, they had never healed from their pain. Pitu remembered what Nuliajuk had told him: "*You must heed each and every single warning.*"

He was trapped.

The spirits converged, all needing him to console them. He had thought that they would be able to console each other, to heal each other. How stupid of him, to think that one could set aside one's own traumas to help another.

They crashed into him, and Pitu fell down. They were crying for healing, crying for love, crying for help, crying for help, crying for help.

Tiri bit Pitu's fingers, trying to pull him out of their grasp, but there was only so much a fox could do against a dozen spirits that needed help.

Pitu pushed them off. He felt sorry for how weak and thin they were. He moved swiftly in an effort to stand up, but the spirits clung to him. Their hands gripped his ankles, pulling him toward them. He had to pull his legs from their grips, running and dodging as the spirits crowded toward him, wanting him.

Tiri barked at the spirits, but they ignored her, just as he had. After a little effort, it didn't matter.

Pitu and Tiri ran out of their reach. They ran toward the crack in the ice but did not dive into it. Instead they ran alongside it, keeping a safe distance away from the jagged and dangerous edge of the water. The spirits tried to keep up, but they were weak and easy to outrun.

Pitu ventured a look behind him and saw that the spirits were out of sight. The two slowed to a rushed walk. Though they could not see the spirits, they could still hear their tragic cries.

Pitu wondered why he'd been washed up here, of all places. The Naglitaujuit were sad and needed his help, he knew that, but why send him here when there was another task he so desperately needed to complete? A whole community struck by famine was waiting for him to return with good news. They expected him to return with animals thrashing in tow.

A thought occurred to him. Perhaps it wasn't so odd that Pitu had been brought here, where helping spirits were supposed to love and heal hurt spirits. The village he was meant to save was haunted by dark spirits that were brought forth by a wronged person.

Dark spirits were not always what they seemed. As Pitu and Tiri rushed away from the sad place, the cries slowly fading to sound like those cold, windy days outside the iglu, things started to come together. He thought of the crying he'd heard when he was drowning, drifting into and out of consciousness. Those cries reminded him of the Naglitaujuit.

If he was so unnerved by and empathetic to those cries, how could a caregiver not be also? Had they heard her cries and gone to help her? Had the Owl helped them, leading the spirits to the one who sought retribution?

16

Return

Pitu and Tiri ran and ran, until they saw a mountain emerge on the horizon. The crack in the ice widened into a familiar polynya. Pitu saw the Owl, sitting at the edge with a fishing lure, jigging it up and down, trying to catch something while waiting. The Owl looked up and saw them approaching and began to pack up its things, wrapping the lure around the caribou-antler handle.

The Owl stood just as Pitu and Tiri reached where it had been sitting. The Owl tilted its head as it had done before, but this time it did not bother Pitu. He was tired, and while the Owl may have been creepy, it was nothing compared to qallupilluit and Naglitaujuit.

"So much has happened to you in so short a time," the Owl said. "It's impressive that you overcame each obstacle."

"I must go back," Pitu said curtly. "There is still a lot of work to be done."

The Owl nodded. "I thought so, but first . . ." The Owl's gaze returned to the open water before them. Curiosity enveloped the space around them, and the Owl asked, "How did you do? Your time below went quicker than most."

How could Pitu describe everything? He had touched Nuliajuk's hair and spoken to her, but his memories of her were already foggy. She had been a presence far too mighty to put into words; then the encounter with the Naglitaujuit had overshadowed the whole experience. Now Pitu thought back. "She was powerful," Pitu answered. "Combing was too much for me. I kept losing my grip and tangling the hair again. I asked to cut her hair with the knife you gave me."

"Ah." The Owl nodded, its curiosity transforming into a small sense of pride. "So, you're one of the few who understood the knife's purpose. Atii. Let's go."

The Owl guided Pitu back through the caves of the mountain. It gave Pitu a moment to change back into his caribou-skin clothing, knowing that on the mortal side of the mountain, the cold was much more real. Pitu peeled the sealskin mask from his face. He shivered with the feeling. He tucked the mask into the hood of his sealskin parka, carefully rolled the sealskin clothes, and tied them up with rope. He brought out the knife, wondering how many shamans took it to the bottom of the sea and did not use it. Pitu gave the knife back to the Owl, who took it without a word. Pitu saw a shift in the mask's expression, a grin filled with mischief and pride.

At the edge of the cave, the Owl stopped before the light from the entrance hit its body. The spirit turned to look back at Pitu. "Good luck, young shaman."

Pitu stepped around, but before leaving, he said to the Owl, "Thank you for all your help. If there is any more trouble in this area, please find a way to tell me. I want to help."

The Owl nodded. "I don't much care for the help of shamans," it said. "And I care much less for helping shamans, but if ever I have need of you, you'll hear from me."

"Keep well," Pitu said, taking the Owl's comments in good humour.

They said goodbye. Pitu stepped outside, into the bright light of the sinking sun. At the campsite, his three partners waited. Ka'lak sat on the qamutiik, crafting some sort of object—a hunting tool, most likely. Tumma was feeding the dogs, teaching Atiq what to do. It took them a moment to realize that Pitu was nearby. Tiri was at his heels, but Pitu knew they could not see her ethereal form.

Atiq ran up to Pitu, excited to see his older brother return. "Big brother!" he called. "You've been gone for so long!"

Pitu asked, "How long?"

Atiq looked back and Tumma said, "Only two nights. Almost three."

Pitu raised his eyebrows. He looked back at the setting sun. "Let's start our way back. We can make it before morning."

The hunters all agreed, and they packed up their camp quickly and seamlessly. Just before leaving, Pitu looked into the iglu, a last check to make sure nothing had been left behind. A sudden urge to destroy the iglu came over him, even though an iglu was usually left intact in case a lost or tired hunter came upon it and needed shelter. Pitu began to take the iglu apart, kicking in the hardened snow walls and pulling out the higher blocks. The others followed his actions, perhaps not understanding why, but trusting Pitu's judgment.

They didn't ask why they had taken down the iglu. Again, Pitu didn't volunteer any information. Telling the hunters might make them nervous. Pitu had little experience in sending spirits away. Destroying the iglu was his way of ensuring that the spirits would make no stops on their way back to where they belonged. He was sure that the spirits in the starving community, once sent away, would meander back in this direction, through the path in the Owl's cave.

As they made their way toward the village, Pitu looked back at the mountain and the remnants of their campsite, seeing the blue light of spirits. He looked again in the direction they were headed. The dogs were swift, making quick progress over the smooth ice.

It was a long, tiring ride back to the village. Atiq was fast asleep on the qamutiik, while Pitu ran alongside the dog team, keeping the lines untangled and directing the dogs ever forward. Ka'lak sat on the other qamutiik, winded but not sleeping. Tumma ran along with his dog team, doing the same thing as Pitu.

The sun had long set. Now the sky was brightening, but Pitu knew that it would still be a long while before the sun came over the horizon.

The village was already awake. Men were preparing hunting equipment while their sons watched with interest. Teenage girls watched their younger siblings play. Pitu knew that mothers and elders sat within their igluit, watching babies and preparing food. As the people saw and heard the approaching dog teams, they gathered to welcome Pitu and the hunters. Aqiggiq, the elderly woman who led this camp, was at the centre of the group, standing slightly ahead of the rest.

The village greeted the return with enthusiasm and excitement. Their heaviness was lifted, but Pitu only felt it upon himself more. He had much more work to do.

"Welcome back," Aqiggiq said joyfully, a smile deepening the wrinkles on her face. Her eyes had disappeared within the folds, reminding Pitu so strongly of his mother. He missed her, and he hoped that she wasn't worrying too much. Aqiggiq asked, "Do you bring good news?"

Everyone was silent, waiting to hear Pitu's tale.

"My work is not done," he said. "Please, everyone must go inside their igluit, and they mustn't leave until I say it is safe."

"What is it?" Aqiggiq asked, worry replacing her joy. "What has happened?"

"I have been to the ocean. I have seen the Woman Below," Pitu said. "But there is more I have to do to appease her. To complete my task, I need everyone to go inside. I need privacy."

Aqiggiq raised her brows. "Atii!" she shouted. "Go inside! Everyone!"

The people listened, slowly making their way back into their igluit. Pitu's hunting party stayed behind a moment, except Ka'lak, who returned to his family. Ijiraq and Qajaarjuaq waited behind, too. Tumma asked, "Do you need any help?"

Pitu scrunched his nose. "You have helped enough already. This is something that I must do alone."

Atiq cried, "Don't go away. Let me stay with you."

"No, little brother," Pitu said, kneeling down to face Atiq. He hugged him tightly, reassuringly. "Don't worry. It won't take long," Pitu said.

Pitu stood, looking at Ijiraq and Qajaarjuaq. He'd almost forgotten about his loathing for the latter, and now a strong uneasiness filled him. Qajaarjuaq paid no attention, instead going to talk to Tumma. Pitu looked at Ijiraq. "Did anything happen while I was away?" His eyes darted quickly toward Qajaarjuaq, implying, *Did he do anything while I was away?*

Ijiraq leaned closer, whispering, "In the daytime, he was helpful. At night, he would sneak women into his iglu. . . . I had started to keep watch outside to make sure he stopped . . . but he started sneaking into others' igluit at night, even when he was not welcome." Ijiraq scrunched his nose, guilt apparent in his voice. "I tried to stop him. No matter what I did to prevent him, he would still find a way to sneak by me. He charmed the people, made them think he was a good man, but women would come to me to tell me what he'd done."

Pitu mirrored the disgust on Ijiraq's face. He sidestepped Ijiraq, rushing toward Qajaarjuaq and grabbing the older man. He pulled him away from

Tumma, making Qajaarjuaq stumble away from the others, away from the igluit. Stragglers not yet within their igluit stopped to watch.

Qajaarjuaq struggled against Pitu's grip, but it was too tight and strong. Anger filled Qajaarjuaq's face. "Let go of me," he growled.

But Qajaarjuaq's anger was nothing compared to Pitu's. Without any consideration, without asking, Pitu said, "Leave this place. Take your dog team, take what is packed on your sled, and leave. Do not go back home. Do not come back."

"You can't just tell me to leave," Qajaarjuaq said. "You may be a shaman, but you have no say over what I do."

"You're lucky I'm letting you have your dogs," Pitu said, his voice incredibly calm. "If you don't leave now, I will make you walk without anything, without equipment, without food."

Qajaarjuaq pulled his arm out of Pitu's grip, an ugly grimace on his face. He said some foul words under his breath, but he listened. He woke his dogs, and he rode off into the growing dawn. There was a pause as they all watched Qajaarjuaq leave. Pitu took long, deep breaths to calm himself down.

"He will probably return to our home," Ijiraq said after a while. "He'll tell lies to Tagaaq and try to turn people against you."

"I don't care," Pitu said. "It doesn't matter. Everyone needs to go inside now. There are bigger things to worry about."

17

Darkness

Once everyone had gone inside, Pitu waited for silence. He waited for everyone to stop talking, to stop trying to listen to figure out what he might be doing outside. He had infinite patience. Pitu waited there without a single movement, taking calm, deep breaths. He stood motionless, just as he would if he were waiting for a seal at a breathing hole. And even though the day had just begun, and the sun had just risen, the people began to fall asleep as they waited.

As the first snores started, Pitu finally moved.

He weaved through the igluit, finding the one glowing with the blue light he'd grown to see more clearly. The spirits, no longer hiding now that they knew he understood why they were here, waited within.

Pitu crawled into the iglu, finding thick darkness inside. Shadows materialized, like clouds of fog. For a moment, he was reminded of the ocean, of treading through its depths. The sun was shining outside and should have been coming through the snow walls, but Pitu couldn't see anything. He opened his eyes wide, trying to see through the thick shadows.

It was freezing inside, colder than it was outside. He shivered in the cold. Even the sound seemed muffled, but he could hear a soft whimpering sound. The air smelled of salt and decay.

The darkness felt familiar. After leaving Nuliajuk's space at the bottom of the sea, after the qallupilluit had tried to drown him, Pitu had woken up to this darkness for a moment. He remembered the helpless, painful cries he had heard. There was nothing he could have done then; there had been water in his lungs, and he couldn't move.

Now, he crawled deeper inside, deeper into the miserable dark. The whimpers grew louder; they grew into the same broken sobs he'd heard after the sculpins had saved him.

"Ikuma," Pitu said, his voice sounding hollow in the dark. "It's me, Piturniq. I'm here."

The cries stopped abruptly with a quick intake of breath. A terrible pause followed, no sound, no light, nothing.

Just as Pitu was going to speak again, a tiny flicker of light appeared in the iglu. Blue light, showing Pitu that he was not alone here with Ikuma. He could barely see her, just the silhouette of her body, her face buried in her hands. She heaved out deep breaths, but he couldn't hear anything.

Pitu crawled closer, the glow becoming slightly brighter with each measure. He could now see more, but Ikuma still had her face buried. He could see her grandmother's motionless frame lying down behind her, and Ikuma's torn clothing.

He crawled close enough that he could reach out and touch her. Pitu did nothing, though; he waited in silence for her to say something, giving her all the power. She deserved that.

Ikuma looked up from her hands. Blackness poured from her eyes. Her tears were shadows, leaking out and causing the darkness within the iglu. The torment on her face was haunting. Pitu was not afraid, though. He was sad. He felt what she felt, but moreover, he felt a bottomless failure, guilt for leaving her when he had known she was troubled and mistreated.

"You're back," she said, her voice so small. The torment woven through her changed, blame taking its place. "You left, and that horrible man stayed."

The black pouring out of her grew thicker, and Pitu could feel it clinging to his skin and body. His disgust came back as he thought of Qajaarjuaq, knowing that he was the horrible man Ikuma was referring to.

"I've sent him away," Pitu said, knowing how feeble that sounded. Words flew out of his mouth as he tried to tell her how badly he felt. "I'm so sorry, Ikuma. I thought that I did enough to stop him, but I failed. I didn't think he would do anything while I was gone. I wanted to protect you, but I left. I should have done something. I'm so sorry."

Ikuma didn't say anything. Her arms had gone limp, defeated. What else could Pitu say? Words meant nothing. Nothing. What had happened, what she had experienced, had already passed. There was nothing he could say or do to change that.

Pitu took his mitts off, holding his hands with his palms up to show Ikuma how much they shook. She looked at them, then at him. Still, she said nothing.

"I am blinded," Pitu said. "I forget that many people are not good people. I forget that pain is more than just getting hurt by accident. I forget that there are many things and actions that people do that I will never understand."

Ikuma reached out. She put her hands into his open palms.

He crawled closer, his hands tightening, squeezing hers softly. Pitu continued, "I forget that promises are so easily broken."

She crumpled into Pitu's arms. He held onto her. She was freezing, trembling from cold and from her cries.

Pitu thought of all the dreams he'd had in the last few weeks. The bright, blinding sunlight, the warmth, the countless animals lending him strength. He wished he could share it with her. He wished he could give it to her. He stroked her arm. "I owe you safety," he said. He thought of the instant connection he had felt with her. He added, "I owe you sunlight.

That is what I felt when I met you. I thought it was just the kindness I felt from you, but there was more to it."

She listened. Still no words.

"It's okay," Pitu said gently. "I understand why . . . I understand why you called the spirits to help you."

Finally, her voice shaking, she spoke. "You know it was me?"

"Yes," Pitu said, "And it's okay."

She sobbed once more, then she climbed out of his embrace, going back to her grandmother's side. Through gasping and shaking breaths, she told Pitu everything. "My grandfather was hurting us. He was hurting my grandmother, and he was beating me. Everyone believed he was a good person. They knew what he did to us, but the people never did anything to stop him. He made sure our village was safe, so they never tried to intervene. I—I just wanted to make them feel how we felt."

Anger filled him, anger at her grandfather and the people in the village. Anger at Aqiggiq for letting a family suffer. Pitu knew that if he'd ever done anything to harm another person, his mother would put him in his place, and Tagaaq would send Pitu away.

Not all villages are the same, not all leaders are the same. He'd grown up in relative comfort. His people had their fair amount of close calls with starvation, with bad people, but they had always overcome them through shared action and responsibility.

He tried to rein in his anger, to make it rational and sympathetic. He understood why the others had never intervened, but it was difficult to accept. Tagaaq had led a community of people with morality, but that was not easy. A lot of the time, people were bystanders, knowing that something was wrong but not knowing how to help.

"I don't know how the spirits came, how they knew, but they appeared one day," Ikuma continued. "They consumed my grandfather. They went into his dreams and ate him from the inside out. They stopped him from hurting us."

"These spirits are caregivers," Pitu said, offering an explanation. "They take care of broken spirits, of people who have experienced pain. They heal them. They accept them. They must have heard you and come to help you."

Ikuma sniffed. "I don't know how to make them leave. They try to protect me, but they couldn't heal my grandmother from her sickness. They couldn't stop that man from coming into my bed at night."

"They are not meant for our world," Pitu answered. "They don't understand how life works and how people are. They only know how to take care of our hurting spirits, not our lives."

Ikuma's crying had stopped. It felt to Pitu as though he could see and feel all her thoughts and emotions in that moment, as though each inhale told him what was wrong. Ikuma didn't need to say anything. She seemed to feel sorry for the trouble she had caused. She wasn't sorry for losing her grandfather. She wasn't sorry for getting the help and protection the spirits temporarily brought. She was only sorry that she did not know how to send them away.

Pitu spoke fervently, "I was sent here to help, to send them away."

She looked at him more directly. Pitu continued his story, the words falling from his mouth as though they were running downhill. "Since my journey here began, I've dreamt of great sunlight, of warm summer days and animals everywhere. I thought it was the spirits trying to persuade me with the lure of great power, but they were giving me the answer."

Pitu opened his palms before him once more, finally understanding. He thought of the dreams, their pure light and goodness. He imagined an orange glow blooming from his hands, washing out the sad blue light. "It wasn't about the power I could hold. It wasn't about the corruption of good shamans. The caregivers were trying to make me understand that it was the power of life that was needed to help you."

The darkness began to fade, shrinking back, leaking through the iglu walls. Outside, the orange light of the risen sun slowly began to come in and overtake the darkness. Pitu reached out, his hands touching Ikuma's cheeks to wipe away the shadows that clung to her. He said, "You have been hurting for too long to know what life felt like . . . you've been thinking of death for a long time, haven't you?"

Ikuma closed her eyes, pressing her lips tightly together.

"It's okay," Pitu said again. "You have been strong for so long."

She opened her eyes. "Every day was a fight," she said, "to take care of myself. To make sure my grandmother stayed alive. I was so alone for so long. Every day, I wanted to leave everyone and everything behind. I walked out of the village almost every single night . . . but I always came back to take care of my grandmother."

The shadows inside were almost gone, the darkness slowly fading. The light eased its way in, revealing the dishevelled interior of the iglu. The qulliq was long burnt out. Stone pots and cooking tools dirty and long untouched. Ikuma's grandmother's body still lay on the bed, appearing to be asleep. Ikuma, still gazing at her grandmother, said, "She died this morning, and I was going to leave tonight. I was going to disappear, but you came back."

The light in the iglu was bright and all-encompassing. The shadows were gone, touching nothing, leaving no darkness behind.

"Your strength has nothing to do with my return," Pitu said. "There is so much of yourself that you do not see. It will take time, but you are the one reason you have survived for so long. Despite everything, you have kept strong."

"But you are the one who helped me," Ikuma said, not quite believing him.

Pitu scrunched his nose. "You are the one who survived, Ikuma. I am only here to witness your strength."

The light had fully returned now, basking in Ikuma's realization. There was still some skepticism within her. Pitu knew this because it looked as though the returned light had skipped over her and she herself was still shrouded in shadow. Pitu knew that those little voices in her mind might take a lifetime to extinguish.

"I was alone for so long," Ikuma said. "I lived alone for so long. Even when my grandparents were alive. I survived alone."

Pitu raised his eyebrows. "Sometimes loneliness is the worst thing we can face. Worse than hunger, worse than loss."

"I don't want to feel alone anymore," Ikuma said, her voice catching on the last word. She looked at her grandmother, touching her arm with affection. "There is nothing for me here anymore."

"Once the animals return," Pitu said, "I will be leaving. I want you to come with me."

Ikuma looked at him again. The sadness was still within her, but a glimmer of hope was there, too. She took hold of his hand, the orange glow finally touching her skin, finally ebbing into her.

The spirits had all left. They hadn't been dark or evil, but they had carried anguish with them wherever they went. Shadows carried over from eons of taking care of those who had been hurt in their lives. That is why Nuliajuk couldn't stand the animals coming back bearing those shadows. They carried the anguish she had found a way to defeat.

"Do you want to come with me?" Pitu asked.

She looked down at their hands. He could see that she was scared, but she nodded. "You've shown more kindness to me than I've felt all my life," she said. "I would like to see where someone like you has come from."

Pitu smiled. Thinking of home, he said, "We would all welcome you."

She laughed, a single tear escaping. No shadows were mixed with her joy now. She looked at her grandmother again. There was grief on her face, but a small smile pulled at her lips. "She would want me to go with you." More tears. Then she said, "We have to bury her before we leave."

Pitu squeezed her hand again. "Yes, of course. We can take all the time you need."

18

Quiet

Together, Pitu and Ikuma wrapped her grandmother in the caribou-skin blankets. Ikuma's crying returned, filled with mourning. Pitu held on to her while she remembered her grandmother. Then, as her cries subsided, he left to get help from Ijiraq and Tumma. The three of them took Ikuma's grandmother from the iglu.

People emerged from their igluit, knowing now that Pitu's work was complete and that the village was safe. Pitu told the men that it was time to hunt. Tumma gathered a small hunting party and they left on his dogsled. The majority of the hunters, including Ijiraq and Atiq, chose to stay behind to help Pitu and the others honour Ikuma's grandmother.

They put her body on Pitu's qamutiik. Ikuma sat beside her grandmother, crying quietly next to the body. The dogs pulled the qamutiik slowly, following as the locals guided them back to the burial ground around a hillside. Together, the whole village gathered rocks to cover the body.

People shared stories about her grandmother with Ikuma. For the first time, they were being kind to her, showing love and support.

At the end of the burial, Ijiraq said he'd teach Atiq some packing tips, and the two left to give privacy to the mourners. Soon others began to disperse, one by one. Pitu and Ikuma were the last at the cairn, the memorial they had built for her grandmother. The two of them walked back to camp together, far enough away from others that any conversation between them wouldn't be overheard. They didn't touch. No hand-holding or arms over each other's shoulders. Ikuma spoke, her voice full of gratitude. "Thank you, Piturniq."

For once, the use of his name didn't bring the

heavy weight of responsibility upon him. Hearing his name come from her made him feel full. His stomach was in knots, and he felt his cheeks blush.

Just as they were reaching camp, the hunting party returned, two seals in tow. The community was full of joy. As soon as the hunters stopped, their families came forward for a taste of the seal.

One of the hunters offered a piece directly to Ikuma. He said, "Sorry about your grandmother."

Ikuma took the piece of meat, thanking him for the gesture.

Pitu's group began to pack up their things, getting ready for the long trek back home. The people of the village came to thank them for all their help, to praise Pitu for his strength. He told them to find him if they ever needed help again.

Ikuma went to her iglu to retrieve her belongings. She said goodbye to the few kind people she had known. Then she came to Pitu, ready to leave.

Pitu exchanged a few last words with Aqiggiq. He told her that the spirits had been brought by her community's indifference to the mistreatment of Ikuma's family. He said, "As long as you all treat each other with respect and keep each other safe, you will not face famine like this again. Once I get home, I will ask a hunting party to return to bring a dog team for you to rebuild your teams." He finished by adding, "Ikuma will be leaving. She will join us."

Aqiggiq, grateful and understanding, shared no judgment. She expressed joy that Ikuma might find a place where she felt belonging and acceptance.

A moment later, Pitu was strapping the last of his supplies to his qamutiik. He made sure Ikuma sat comfortably on the sled, and then he whistled, signalling the dogs to start walking. Their journey home began. Ijiraq and Tumma led with a dog team, while Pitu, Ikuma, and Atiq followed behind.

19

Nanuq

P itu took a long, deep breath. They had just stopped
for the night. Atiq, naturally, went ahead to check
on the dogs after the long day of running, while Ijiraq
and Tumma went straight to building a couple of
shelters for the night. Pitu unpacked seal meat from
his sled and began to cut pieces for each of them to eat.

Ikuma, unsure of what to do, simply sat on
the qamutiik. She watched the men as they worked
on their respective tasks, flowing from one to the next
without speaking. Pitu snuck glances at her, seeing that
she was engrossed in the work they put into setting
up camp for the night. Miki, fed and ready for rest,
went toward Ikuma. The husky sniffed Ikuma's hand,
startling the girl. Realizing that it was only one of the
dogs, Ikuma reached out to pat the animal.

Once the igluit were built, the dogs had gone
to sleep, and everyone's bellies were full, a thought
occurred to them all. Where would the woman sleep?

Ijiraq and Tumma mumbled something about
needing to find a spot to colour the snow before they
walked away, leaving Pitu and Ikuma alone. Atiq was
already sleeping inside one of the igluit.

Pitu started by asking, "Do you want me to
build you another iglu?" He cleared his throat. "Just
for you?"

"No," Ikuma smiled, scrunching her nose,
"but maybe I could share with Atiq." Pitu agreed. The
suggestion made more sense than the work of building
another iglu. There were still certain customs that
needed to be upheld, especially after what they had all
just gone through. A married man and two unmarried
men could not share an iglu with an unmarried
woman. Atiq, on the other hand, was young enough

that the taboo would not be broken. Ikuma yawned and stretched. "I think I'm going to go to sleep now, if that's okay."

Pitu said goodnight and let her go. He went into the other iglu, soon to be joined by Ijiraq and Tumma.

That night, Pitu dreamt of absolutely nothing. There were no glorious fields bursting with thousands of grazing caribou, no floe edges with whales and other sea mammals swimming in abundance. He had simply closed his eyes and, hours later, opened them well rested and ready for a day of travelling.

The trip home seemed to be much shorter than their journey to the village. Perhaps that was because Qajaarjuaq was not there to complain anymore, or because they were impatient to return. As it was, the easy nature of the group made the days feel shorter, the day's work less exhausting. The land grew more and more familiar as they saw places where they'd previously gone hunting. After a couple of weeks of travelling, Pitu could see that they were only about a day or two away from home.

In the morning, it took almost no time to pack up their camp. If they were swift, they could make it home by that night. They followed a fading trail left by a dog team. Pitu suspected that the trail belonged to Qajaarjuaq. He made a point to remember that he would have to stop and tell Ikuma about the likelihood of running into Qajaarjuaq and brace her for that encounter.

By midday, in addition to the dog team trail, they had spotted polar bear tracks. They stopped the qamutiit, checking to see how fresh the tracks were. There were probably two bears, a mother and an older cub. The tracks were new and recent, following the dog team that had come this way before them. Pitu's group knew they might catch up to the bears on their journey, or to Qajaarjuaq harvesting them.

Up ahead, the land was just beginning to change. They were no longer travelling along the coastline on smooth lengths of ice. Instead the terrain turned into a range of hills, spotted with dark rocks against the white snow, with the tops of summer plants peeking out as they hibernated beneath. They ventured into the beginnings of cracked, rugged ice. Their pace slowed as they approached the rough terrain ahead.

Their pace had slowed considerably, but they kept moving without stopping. As they travelled through the coastal ice, they hit a few bumps—the dogs slipped on the ice and were hurt by the qamutiik, supplies packed into the sled came loose and fell off, having to be retrieved. At one point Ikuma, not used to travelling and unsure of whether to stay on the qamutiik or to jump off while going over a particularly steep and slippery patch of ice, fell off the sled and hurt her shoulder.

All the while, they worried that a polar bear would appear around every corner. Tracks showed the polar bears roaming throughout the area, going over the same cracks, turning around the same corners. At one point, the hunters came across what was left of a seal, the last bits of its flesh being scavenged by foxes. Hopefully that meant the bears wouldn't be hungry and would ignore the hunters if they were to encounter each other.

Pitu felt a strong sense of relief when they left the jagged ice behind for the hills. The dogs continued up the hillside. Atiq and Ijiraq went ahead with the dogs, while Pitu and Tumma checked on Ikuma's shoulder to make sure she was okay. When she brushed them off, saying she was fine, they went ahead and walked the rest of the way up the hill.

At the top, the dogs were resting and Ijiraq was cutting up meat for them to eat. While chewing on the meat, Pitu looked out at the path ahead. He could see the shapes of the hills, some rising as if they were sleeping giants. In one of those valleys and fjords would be their home, and their families.

For a fleeting moment, Pitu thought about Saima and how she might feel seeing Ikuma with them. He felt a sharp ache in his stomach, guilt mixing with a question he was all too familiar with. *What if?* The question hadn't left him for months, but now he felt at peace with it. He looked at Ikuma, not quite sure where their relationship would go, but knowing now that he could have a life and find kinship with someone other than Saima.

Their rest was short-lived. They kept moving, down the hill and through the valleys and over more hills. The polar bear tracks had left them uncomfortable, to the point that they had begun pushing the dogs too hard.

It was a while before they finally stopped in order to give the dogs time to truly rest. Everyone was tired and anxious, hoping it wouldn't take much longer to get home. They did what they usually did when stopping for a break: they ate and shared stories.

Pitu was finally ready to share details of the journey he'd just taken. He didn't speak of Nuliajuk; he would save that story for another time. Right now, she was still a memory gone vague, her presence too incomprehensible to put into words. Instead, Pitu told them about the Owl, the spirit's collection of masks, and the way it spoke. "Every time the Owl spoke, it tilted it's head, like this—" Pitu mimicked the movement and laughed in the same creepy chuckle.

Atiq made a whiny sound. "Eeee, don't do that!"

The others looked at Atiq and then all copied the movement and laugh Pitu had just shown. All four of them tilted their heads, chuckled, and for added effect Tumma said, "What's wrong, Atiq?"

As usual, Atiq began to cry. Everyone laughed, finding amusement in the little boy's terror before they went on to comfort him a moment later.

Pitu didn't want to worry them by recounting the other things he seen on his journey. There was enough to worry about. He didn't want Atiq to know that the qallupilluit continued to stalk him, or the hopeless gloom of the Naglitaujuit. He hoped the caregivers had returned and were nurturing them back to health and acceptance.

Ijiraq stood and stretched, taking a few steps away, apart from the group. Pitu noticed his expression furrowed in worry, and he realized that he had not had time to talk to Ijiraq about what had happened while Pitu had been away. Pitu stood, following Ijiraq.

They walked a short distance away, far enough to have a private conversation. Ijiraq had been quiet since telling Pitu what Qajaarjuaq had done. Something was still troubling him, Pitu knew. Perhaps it was the same feeling that Pitu had had when he was in Ikuma's dark iglu the day before, the guilt of having failed someone.

Pitu patted Ijiraq on the back, a small offering of comfort. Ijiraq nodded, but his furrowed brow did not relax. Sounding discouraged and ashamed, he said, "I could have done better. I could have done more."

They were the same words Pitu had said to Ikuma—words of guilt from a man unsure how to move on. Truthfully, they were some of the most meaningless words that anyone could say, and Pitu recognized now that what he had said the day before may have been just as worthless. They were throwaways, words to show that one felt bad, but nothing else. They took the attention, the care, away from the person who deserved it. These words shut a person into the idea that there was nothing else he could do. Acknowledging that he hadn't done the right thing at the time was one thing, it was an admirable thing, but it was still nothing. Pitu mirrored Ijiraq's anguish, sighing and shaking his head, too.

"It happened," Pitu said. "Even if there was more that could have been done to prevent something from happening, you cannot go back and change anything."

"What am I supposed to do?" Ijiraq said, finding no comfort in the shaman's words. "I feel terrible. What am I supposed to do with this feeling?"

At first, Pitu simply shrugged, saying, "What can you do? I feel the same way. I don't really have the answers."

A solemn quiet came over them, both men pondering their incompetence. They stood with their hands on their hips, looking toward the path they would soon follow. It was only a matter of time before they would reach home, catching up to the perpetrator of these vile acts. It was clear now that Qajaarjuaq would return to their village—perhaps he had already arrived—to tell lies to Tagaaq and to Pitu's mother and to Saima. Pitu was sure that no one would believe Qajaarjuaq, and once they caught up to tell the truth, they would be rid of the despicable man for good.

Their silence grew uncomfortable. Pitu thought of their first night all those weeks ago, the first true conversation that Pitu and Ijiraq had. At the time, Pitu had no trust or good feeling for Ijiraq. Now, he had grown to respect the man greatly.

Finally, Pitu shrugged once more. He said, "I suppose we must carry these feelings with us until we grow from them. We can feel bad all we want, but it doesn't mean anything until we take the responsibility to grow past it and prevent it from happening again in the future."

Ijiraq looked at Pitu, his brow still furrowed. "Did you just think of that," he said, "or did you get that from somewhere?"

"I just thought of it now," Pitu said, a grin crossing his face.

Ijiraq raised his eyebrows, finally releasing them from being furrowed for such a long time. An impressed whistle came from his mouth. "Sometimes you're smarter than you seem."

They both laughed, turning to walk back to the group. The feeling wasn't gone, but they could worry about it another time, once they were home and with their loved ones. They still had roaming bears to worry over, and a young child and woman to keep safe.

Tumma had already gotten the dogs ready for the next, and hopefully last, leg of the journey. As soon as Pitu and Ijiraq were back, they got ready to go, Tumma and Ijiraq taking the lead while Atiq, Pitu, and Ikuma followed behind. The dogs were steady, eager to return home, too.

The sky had long darkened, but Pitu could see familiarity in the landscape. An old campground, inuksuit built by other hunters, the shapes of hills he knew well. The dogs had begun to run faster, knowing that they were almost home. The slowest dog, which usually ran right next to the qamutiik, picked up speed, using up the energy it had been saving all that time. The last dog bit the haunches of the others, making them pick up their pace, too.

The valleys had begun to narrow, a steep and jagged cliff on one side of them and a rocky hill on the other. Up ahead, Tumma made a sound—a soft grunt that echoed the coo of a raven—that made the dogs' ears perk up in attention. It seemed they had finally caught up to the polar bear that had been following Qajaarjuaq's path. Tumma, with his focus set on the horizon, had spotted the beast before anyone else.

The dogs quickened again. They stopped close enough to try to intimidate the bear, but still a safe distance away. Pitu could see one bear near the cliff's edge, its jaw tearing at the carcass of a frozen seal. The state of the seal confused Pitu. Polar bears usually ate freshly caught seal, hardly leaving enough time for the body to freeze or saving it for later. Had the bear stumbled upon the seal? If so, who had left it? Had all the other seal remains they'd seen been left behind and frozen, too? An uneasy feeling gathered in Pitu's guts. He wondered if Qajaarjuaq had left the carcasses to attract bears and make their journey more difficult.

Tumma released his slowest dog out of its harness, knowing that the dog still had enough saved energy to distract the bear and evade its pursuit. The polar bear had turned toward them to defend itself. The dog rushed around the bear, biting the bear's hindquarters as it would its dog teammates, and darted through its legs to hide underneath it. Confused and distracted, the bear focused its attention on the dog, trying to swipe at it but not flexible enough to reach the dog hiding under it.

While Tumma held the harnesses of the other dogs to calm them and keep them from harm, Ijiraq had a bow and arrow in his hands, the bowline taut as he carefully aimed toward the bear. Pitu was keeping grip of his own team, using all his strength to keep them at bay.

Ijiraq walked toward the bear, aiming carefully and making sure the arrow would have enough force. The dog was distracting enough that the bear didn't notice the hunter's approach. As the bear rose to stand on its hind legs out of annoyance at the dog, Ijiraq loosened the arrow with finesse. It landed true in the bear's chest, piercing straight through to its heart.

The dog ran to escape as the polar bear fell. It was then that they realized another bear had been on the other side of the valley, hiding between the boulders to eat another seal in privacy. Now the bear was running with full force toward them. The free dog had run straight toward it, but this bear was much larger, and it had seen the other bear killed. As the dog tried to round the bear to slide under its belly, the bear swiped a huge paw and hit the dog with the force of pure muscle and weight. The dog flew, its breath whining from its lungs. The dog, dazed, stayed on the ground.

There was no stopping the bear. Pitu released his grip on the harnesses, shouting, "Atiq, give me my spear!"

The polar bear barrelled straight toward Ijiraq. The hunter had no time to react, no time to notch another arrow before the bear hit him and began to maul him. Atiq had tossed the spear to Pitu, then dove to restrain the dog harnesses. Pitu told Ikuma to let their slower dog out of its harness so that it might distract the bear, then ran toward the bear and Ijiraq with his harpoon raised. He didn't know if the dog was successful, for he had reached the bear first, and he struck his spear into its ribs.

The bear lunged toward him, its sharp claws reaching for him. Pitu leaned out of reach, taking his spear with him. A dog had rushed into the fight, biting into the back of the bear and hurrying underneath, just as it had been trained to do. The bear, temporarily distracted, stumbled against the dog. Pitu thrust his spear once more, striking the bear in his throat.

The bear fell, dead. Pitu rushed to Ijiraq, the hunter bordered between two bears. He didn't even know whether Ijiraq was alive. Tumma had let go of his dog team to check on Ijiraq, too. They could see that he was breathing, but he was covered in deep gashes and his own blood.

"Ijiraq," Pitu said, his voice shaking. "Ijiraq."

He had no words.

Ijiraq took a breath, tears seeping from his eyes, and coughed. His voice hoarse and frantic, Ijiraq said, "Don't—let—me—die. Don't—let—me—"

There was a cut so deep in Ijiraq's cheek that Pitu didn't know what to do or say. Ikuma had reached them, pushing past Pitu to put clean snow into the cuts. Ijiraq screamed against the stinging cold, but he didn't fight against her.

She instructed the others what to do. Tumma went to retrieve items from his qamutiik: extra skins they had brought, medicinal plants collected in the warmth of summer, and the fat from seals and whales. She cleaned Ijiraq's wounds while the hunter cried against each touch. She wrapped skins against his wounds to ebb the blood flow.

Atiq had reinserted the free dog into its harness and brought Pitu's dog team as close to them as he could. Pitu and Tumma carried Ijiraq—the man screaming against each movement—onto the sled. Without hesitation, Pitu took off, knowing that the others would recover the things Pitu had left behind, check on the dog that the polar bear had hurt, and follow closely behind. Once they arrived at their village, they'd send a hunting party to find the bodies of the bears and bring them back for harvesting.

The dogs ran harder than they ever had. Miki led without reluctance, the boss dog in the middle didn't let any of the other dogs get out of line or tangled up, and the slow dog that was actually not slow at all urged the others to run ever faster with nips at their hindquarters.

Pitu's feet couldn't keep up, and he soon had to sit on the qamutiik so he wouldn't be left in their wake. Ijiraq had screamed with each movement, but soon his throat was either too raw or his pain had dulled so much that he could no longer feel it. Pitu could see Ijiraq's blood in the dim moonlight, bleeding through the skins Ikuma had strapped tightly over his wounds.

Pitu looked at Ijiraq's face, seeing that his mouth was moving. Pitu moved down, putting his ear close to Ijiraq's mouth. "Piturniq," Ijiraq said, barely loud enough to be heard over the dogs.

"Huh?" Pitu said.

Ijiraq laughed deliriously. "You're the ijiraq from my mother's dream."

Pitu remembered the story, the reason behind Ijiraq being named after a creature typically known for being malicious.

"Maybe I died in my mother's dream," Ijiraq said. "And she just didn't tell me."

"You're not going to die," Pitu said firmly.

"*Hiiguuq?*" Ijiraq said, his hysteria growing. "You wanna bet?"

Pitu couldn't bring himself to humour the man. His throat was blocked by emotion. If he had made any response, he knew he would begin to cry. They would be home soon.

Pitu looked at his friend, seeing that Ijiraq's laughter had changed to sobs.

20

Home Again

It seemed like no time at all before they saw the glowing igluit of their families and friends. The dogs barked and howled at the sight, alerting the villagers of their arrival. Pitu could see that people had already emerged from their domed houses to meet another hunter returning from the same journey. They had caught up to Qajaarjuaq.

A small sense of frustration bubbled up inside Pitu at the sight of Qajaarjuaq. He stored the frustration away for now, instead wanting to focus all energy on the wounded Ijiraq, who had stopped talking, laughing, and crying altogether. The man stared blankly at the sky. The only indication that he was alive was his shallow breathing. Pitu tried to alert him that they were home, but Ijiraq made no acknowledgment of hearing or understanding.

The gathered crowd stole their attention away from Qajaarjuaq as Pitu and his dog team slowed to a stop. Pitu spotted his mother, Inuuja, and Tagaaq almost immediately. Pitu shouted, "*Ikajuqtaulanga!*" over and over again. "Help me!"

Joy at the arrival quickly changed to looks of worry as the crowd realized that something was wrong with Ijiraq. Two women, an elder named Qaunaq and a woman named Aksaajuq, surged through the crowd of onlookers. Qaunaq was known to be the best in camp at mending and healing wounds, and she was teaching her daughter-in-law to follow in her footsteps. Immediately, they began to order for help to move Ijiraq.

Ijiraq grunted as he was moved, finally breaking his silence. Saima pushed through to see what the commotion was. A horrified gasp mixed with a sob ripped out of her throat at the sight. She tried to move toward Ijiraq, then stopped, as if second-guessing herself. Ijiraq heard her outburst and moved his head to look at her. Their eyes locked. He made a strangled sound, and Saima went to her husband. She followed the men who were moving Ijiraq's wounded and mauled body to be mended in an iglu nearby. Pitu had no doubt that it was Saima's iglu they were going into.

A pitiful feeling filled Pitu as he recognized a pathetic urge to go to Saima, to comfort her, his feelings for her returning with instant fervour. Pitu tore his gaze away from the group. Guilt flowered in his stomach as he thought of Ikuma. The feelings he had for Saima, he knew, might never subside, never leave him completely.

Once Ijiraq was gone, the sight of his mangled body no longer a distraction, the crowd focused back on Pitu.

Pitu's mother came toward him, falling into his embrace. She murmured words full of love and joy to him, glad he had returned safely. Others came forward to greet him, too. His young sister, Arnaapik, his older brother, Natsivaq, and his *puukuluk*, his birth mother, Akumalik. Other family members, cousins, uncles, and aunties all came to see him.

Tagaaq came forward. "Piturniq," Tagaaq said, "where are the others?"

Inuuja let him go, as if only noticing now that her youngest son, Atiq, was not among them. She asked where he was, her look of happiness changing to worry.

"They are coming," Pitu said. "We were attacked by two polar bears. As soon as we put Ijiraq on the qamutiik, I continued the journey home without slowing or stopping."

Most of the people were satisfied with this answer, their gazes shifting to the horizon, trying to catch a glimpse of the next party to arrive.

Tagaaq came forward to embrace Pitu. "I am happy for your safe return."

Before leaving camp all those weeks ago, Tagaaq had looked close to death, had barely been able to stand up. Now, his health seemed to have returned. He looked sturdy. "You're in good health, Uncle," Pitu remarked.

Tagaaq laughed, his familiar smile with missing teeth filling Pitu with a warm feeling of belonging.

The cry of approaching dogs alerted them to the arrival of the last group. Pitu was overcome with relief. His mind had prioritized his panic over Ijiraq, so that he hadn't realized he feared for the others, feared that other creatures had shown up after he'd left.

When they stopped, Atiq ran to his mother. Atiq had grown, Pitu was realizing now. He'd grown to be as tall as Anaana. The two, an elderly mother and her youngest adopted son, clung to each other with a love and affection Pitu hadn't seen very often between them. Atiq had always been preoccupied with childish things, while Pitu and Arnaapik had been helping Anaana take care of the youngest. Though Pitu knew how much the two cared for each other, neither showed it very much. Their vast age difference made it difficult for them to communicate as well as Anaana and her older children did.

Pitu went to help Tumma with the dogs, letting them loose so they could lope off to sleep away their exhaustion from the bear attack and the subsequent flight back to the village. "How is Ijiraq?" Tumma asked.

"I'm not sure," Pitu answered. "They just took him into an iglu with Qaunaq."

Just then, Pitu remembered there was someone new in their group. He turned back to the crowd, looking for Ikuma. She was standing apart from everyone, her gaze turned down to the ground. The crowd was looking at her, wondering who she might be.

Pitu rushed closer, knowing that Qajaarjuaq was somewhere among them. "Ai, this is Ikuma," Pitu began. "She is from the starving village. I brought her here to become a part of our community."

Tagaaq came and offered Ikuma a hand in welcome. Still staring at the ground, she tentatively outstretched her hand to shake. "We welcome you, Ikuma," Tagaaq said.

Others came forward to welcome her.

Pitu searched the crowd for Qajaarjuaq, but he was nowhere to be seen. No doubt he had gone away to hide from Pitu and the others. For all his harsh criticism and feigned masculinity, Qajaarjuaq was nothing more than a coward.

The community members had all gathered into the qaggiq at the centre of their village. Ikuma now sat on one of the snow benches with Inuuja and Arnaapik. Atiq was sitting on the hard-packed snow floor between their legs. Tiri sat in between Pitu's legs, invisible to everyone but him. Tagaaq and Pitu sat directly across from the main entrance of the qaggiq. Before them, Qajaarjuaq strode in, led by Tagaaq's wife, Taina. She held his hand tightly, for the man was her youngest son. Once they were in the centre of the crowded qaggiq, she kissed her son's cheek, tears seeping from her eyes. She left him there, walking over to sit next to her husband.

If there was anything Pitu could find redeemable about the man before him, it was that Qajaarjuaq was silent for once in his life. The usual grimace on his face was gone. He stared blankly at the ground, tears falling from his eyes in salty streaks.

Pitu looked around, seeing shame on most faces. After the worry over Ijiraq had subsided and the community had welcomed Pitu and his hunters back, they had asked why Qajaarjuaq had returned before everyone else.

There had been no need to avoid the subject. Pitu told everyone that he'd tried to exile Qajaarjuaq in order to punish him for his wrongdoings, for all the rules he had broken while they'd been away. Though Pitu couldn't have been sure, he had thought he could see looks of understanding on many of the faces. Someone in the crowd then said that Qajaarjuaq had been misbehaving and abusing others for much longer than just in the time they'd been away.

Quite quickly, everyone had made their way into their large communal iglu. It was as if there had been a collective decision about what needed to happen to confront Qajaarjuaq and have him face the things he'd done, the pain and trauma he had been causing for years. Tagaaq had said, "We must gather." Now they were here.

If they hadn't known before, most people in the community had an idea of why they were now gathered. Qajaarjuaq had done horrible things to find himself there, and now it was up to everyone to hear the story and decide how it would end. Interspersed throughout the crowd were his victims, both recent and from the past, men and women he'd abused over time. For a moment, Pitu was reminded of the Owl and its inclinations toward retribution. He could feel that the room was full of that very same desire.

"Qajaarjuaq, my son," Tagaaq began. There was no pain in his voice, no shaking. The calm that the elder displayed was infallible. "Why have we found you here?"

Qajaarjuaq said nothing.

Impatience overtook some of the onlookers. A voice called out, "He must be sent away! We are not safe if he continues to stay without punishment."

Murmurs of agreement spread through the qaggiq. Pitu could hear sniffling on the other side of Tagaaq. He looked over, seeing the tears fall from Taina's eyes. He saw her deep breaths full of motherly love. Even a man who had done what Qajaarjuaq had could still find love from another person.

As the whispers began to die out, another voice began to tell of Qajaarjuaq's actions. Tumma stood, not looking much younger than Qajaarjuaq anymore. He spoke, "On our journey to the starving people of the Nuvuk area, Qajaarjuaq was a disgraceful tag-along. He complained about everything, refused to treat the rest of us with dignity, and he abused women in Nuvuk."

"Not only in Nuvuk," a woman's voice called out. The people shifted their gazes, looking at the woman who had spoken. She wore a dishevelled amauti, two young children clinging to her arms and legs. Pitu recognized her as Ivalu, one of Qajaarjuaq's wives. "For years he has been leaving Aasivak and I to take care of our children. He gives us barely enough food to feed ourselves, and we have to beg for help from him. When he finally comes back after leaving us for weeks, he only stays long enough to impregnate one of us again. If we try to leave him, to tell him never to come back, he hits us in front of the children."

Other voices told stories of pain at Qajaarjuaq's hand. The number of claims being laid out in the open was more than anyone had thought. How could one man leave such a wake of misery?

"That man," said Saima, her voice shaking with emotion and anger. She was pointing at Qajaarjuaq. Someone had fetched Saima to tell her about the trial they were about to have. She had gone straight to Pitu and asked how there could have been polar bears on their path when the animals always tried to avoid hunters. Pitu had only told her about all the strange seal remains they'd found, and without another word, she'd decided what she thought. Her belief echoed his thoughts from earlier. She said, "I believe he left the bodies of seals along his path as he made his way back home. Polar bears were attracted to the seals, and they attacked our returning shaman and hunters. My husband is dying because of his immaturity and carelessness!"

She broke down, sobbing. Saima's mother wrapped her arms around her daughter's shoulders.

A quiet voice spoke up next, but no one could hear her over the din of crying and accusations. Pitu heard her, though. He had grown to find calm in that voice, to find affection. Pitu shushed the crowd, letting Ikuma's voice be heard.

Quietly, hardly loudly enough to be heard over one's own breath, she told her story. "In Nuvuk, I had been walking back to my grandmother's iglu at night, when everyone else was sleeping. I wasn't paying attention as I crawled inside, only to find that he had followed me in. He . . . he . . . ."

But Ikuma didn't say what happened next. She cried in such a way that she couldn't talk and could only breathe in short gasps. Pitu saw his mother hold Ikuma. He saw the young girl hesitate against such overt affection and care, then bury her face into Anaana's neck.

Qajaarjuaq remained motionless and silent. He hadn't looked up as everyone spoke their piece, and when Tagaaq asked, "Why have you done these things? What do you have to say for yourself?" Qajaarjuaq remained still.

Tagaaq waited, but his son was not going to answer the question. He continued to stare down, avoiding the gazes of his people. Tagaaq shook his head. "I am disappointed in you, Qajaarjuaq. I am sickened. My own son committed these atrocities! What kind of son are you? What kind of man are you?"

A murmur escaped from Qajaarjuaq's lips. The others could not hear. They did not see his mouth move, but Tiri was there. She echoed the words to Pitu: "_It is you who disappoints me._"

Something about this specific interaction made Pitu more uncomfortable. The victims of Qajaarjuaq's vile actions and immorality had, of course, discomforted him. However, the way Tagaaq spoke to his son, and Qajaarjuaq's response to it, were also troubling.

He thought of Nuliajuk. He thought of the Naglitaujuit. He thought of Ikuma.

Life is a cycle; that was something Tagaaq had told Pitu months ago. Violence begat violence. What could that mean in this instance? Where did Qajaarjuaq learn this behaviour?

Perhaps it was too much to bind the behaviour to Tagaaq, but there was no denying that the father-and-son relationship had a place in everything. To Pitu, that was clear now. No one else had seen it, including Pitu, until now. They all had been blinded by their love of Tagaaq and his leadership. No one had thought that he might be a negligent father. No one had thought that Qajaarjuaq had been trying, in some way, to overcome his feelings of never being good enough for a man who was kind and open to everyone but his own son. They never thought that Qajaarjuaq's actions might have stemmed from feelings of constant disapproval and shame.

But this was not enough to forgive Qajaarjuaq his abuses.

There were more stories untold. Pitu could see that among the people. Not everyone wanted to speak, to lay out their vulnerability and pain in front of the whole village. They didn't have to. Pitu wouldn't want to ask that of anyone.

"Qajaarjuaq, I think it is clear," Pitu spoke, "that there is no way you can stay with us. You have hurt us more than we can heal."

There was utter silence as Pitu spoke.

"But, life is and always has been a cycle," he continued. "We are the results of our own experiences, and no one is inherently a bad person. They are brought to this point, and they either overcome those behaviours or they perpetuate them forward."

Pitu looked over at Tagaaq, seeing all the good in his funny and wise uncle. Something lay underneath, however, a small thing that had large consequences. Tiri whispered all that the spirits were saying into Pitu's ear, things about the elder that only the unseen knew. Tagaaq had neglected Qajaarjuaq as the boy grew up. He'd left his son to learn without a mentor. He had laughed at his mistakes.

"Uncle," Pitu began, turning his body so that he could face Tagaaq. The elder turned his own gaze to Pitu's. Pitu swore he heard everyone's hearts stop, the breath in their lungs freeze. "You have moulded my cousin to be this way."

Angry accusations flew out of everyone's mouths, accusing Pitu of stupidity, of absurdity. Pitu raised his hand, palm open, to silence them.

"You made this happen," Pitu continued, feeling the anger palpable in the air. "Due to negligence, due to dismissal of your role as Qajaarjuaq's father. It was your role to teach him how to overcome his struggles, how to process his feelings and learn from his mistakes, how to be held accountable. But you ignored that. You ignored him. You let him do whatever he pleased, then you judged him without telling him what he was doing was wrong. You let him grow up thinking that he could do nothing to get a reaction from you or anyone else. And when he did get a reaction, the behaviour worsened because he felt threatened."

Tagaaq said nothing, but there was no hostility toward Pitu coming from the elder. Tagaaq seemed to find truth in what Pitu was saying.

Pitu turned his attention back to Qajaarjuaq. "Qajaarjuanngai," he said in understanding. Now that his anger was misted by a tiny sense of empathy, he wanted to reassure his cousin with that small term of endearment. Qajaarjuaq was a bad man and needed to be punished, but he was also Pitu's cousin. He was Taina and Tagaaq's son. Though Pitu would have no regret in the decision he chose, he felt that he needed Qajaarjuaq to at least know that his life could have been different. He could have been a good man if he had been greeted with endearment in his life; as Pitu had, as Natsivaq had, as Atiq had as well. A small endearment can change the life of a young man, Pitu realized.

He continued, "You can no longer live here, and you cannot move on to a new village.

"Your father must take you to a new camp, where you will live in solitude. No dog team, only the tools you need to survive and hunt for yourself. Once each season, I will send Tagaaq to check on you. Your dog team will go to Nuvuk, to help their hunters rebuild their own teams."

The crowd murmured, finding good and bad in this punishment. Saima spoke, anger shaking her voice. "Why not just send him away and have him out of our lives for good? Why send Tagaaq to check on Qajaarjuaq to make sure he lives?"

Months ago, Tagaaq had told Pitu about the *Nagliktaujuit* and their land of sorrow and healing. Pitu had seen it with his own eyes. Those souls, the Nagliktaujuit, were broken beyond repair.

Pitu answered, "I have no love or pity for Qajaarjuaq, but I love my Uncle Tagaaq. If he doesn't atone for letting this happen, he will wander in the afterlife. He will never find peace."

There weren't any objections to what Pitu had said. Only more mumblings, children asking their parents what was happening, confused and frustrated shakes of the head. Tagaaq pressed his lips together. Then he smiled in self-deprecation. No humour, just humility.

"I do believe you are right, Piturniq," Tagaaq said, tears now glistening in his eyes. The whispers silenced as the community let Tagaaq speak, surprised that he was not countering what Pitu had mandated. "Our sufferings can move through us. From our grandparents and our parents, through us to our children, to our grandchildren. We are where it needs to stop, not begin. I am sorry that I let my son hurt so many people. Most of all, I am sorry that I hurt him. I accept these conditions," Tagaaq finished.

Pitu, his attention going back to the man standing in the centre of the qaggiq, asked, "What about you, Qajaarjuaq?"

In a meek voice, still staring at the ground, Qajaarjuaq only asked, "Let me go alone."

Pitu scrunched his nose. "No."

Perhaps in death, Qajaarjuaq would not become a Nagliktaujuq. He wasn't broken hearted about all he had done; he wasn't going to think about the ignorance of his father to the point of never healing. Pitu knew that, and he knew that Tagaaq wouldn't, either. There were other creatures in the spirit world, there were other things that they could become. Life carried on in its everlasting struggle, and death did not change one into something unrecognizable. Qajaarjuaq had little good within him, and Pitu did not know what that would mean once he'd perished in this life and was on to the next, to the spirit world. Perhaps Qajaarjuaq would simply move on, but the little that Pitu could do to prevent another dark spirit, he would do.

Softly, Qajaarjuaq said, "I accept these conditions."

Many did not understand why Pitu chose to do what he did. People left in angry huffs, one of whom was Saima. Ikuma lingered, an expression of confusion and betrayal upon her face. She did not speak to Pitu, instead waiting for Anaana to take her out of the qaggiq.

Pitu remained sitting next to Tagaaq. The old man did not seem angry. He did not seem guilty. Tagaaq kept his integrity, his humility.

"It will take some time for them to forgive you," Tagaaq remarked.

Qajaarjuaq still stood in the centre of the qaggiq, but now Taina was embracing him. They held on to each other with relief and affection.

"I have lots of time," Pitu said.

———————

As Tagaaq prepared to take Qajaarjuaq away, Pitu went to see his family. They were all sitting in Anaana's iglu, eating a slab of *maktaaq*, narwhal skin. Atiq was cutting up small, bite-sized pieces and handing them to Natsivaq's young children, while Arnaapik was using an *ulu* to cut pieces and offering them to Ikuma.

Ikuma tried to fit in with the light air of Pitu's family, but the heartbreak was still drawn all over her. She looked up at Pitu, the same expression of disappointment on her face.

Pitu knelt down to join his family. He was ravenous. The family ate together in their easy-going nature. Natsivaq lightheartedly teased his younger brothers, while the children made small cries to be fed more. Pitu's birth mother, Akumalik, breastfed the youngest child, while Anaana tried to teach Ikuma everyone's name and relations, both adopted and biological.

Tumma briefly joined in their feast, coming in for a few bites of maktaaq before asking to speak to the shaman. Pitu stole a quick glance at Arnaapik, only to find her focused wholeheartedly on cutting up more maktaaq for her siblings.

Outside, Tumma told Pitu that the first couple of hunters from the hunting party that had been sent to harvest the polar bear bodies were returning. Tagaaq and Qajaarjuaq had just left. "I am going to bring Qajaarjuaq's dog team to Nuvuk in a couple of days," Tumma said. "Some other hunters will accompany me."

"Okay," Pitu said. "That sounds good."

"I went to check on Ijiraq," Tumma finished off, adding, "Saima wants to see you."

He left Pitu with that invitation, off to take a well-deserved rest. Pitu stood there for a moment, thinking of Saima. He thought of how long it had taken for his feelings for her to dull, only to instantly resurface the moment he'd seen her. He went back into the iglu for a second, asking if Ikuma would follow him.

A minute later, they were outside. For a moment, they simply faced each other. Ikuma's silence, for the first time since they met, wasn't out of timidity. She was angry. Pitu offered, "I hope you will understand someday."

"I don't understand," she said sharply. He shrugged, waiting for her to carry on. Finally, she said, "But I trust you."

Pitu offered his open palms in a gesture of surrender. Ikuma looked into his face, her scrutinizing gaze changing into a half-grin. They hugged then, and Pitu realized it was one of the first times they had really touched since Nuvuk. His affection for her swelled.

"Come," Pitu said. "I want you to meet someone."

He led her to an iglu he had come to avoid before the journey to Nuvuk. He could sense the grief inside. Pitu knew that Ikuma could feel it, too. As he knelt down, about to crawl inside, she tugged his arm. He looked back, and she was shaking her head.

Pitu tilted his head back in a nod, offering a look of reassurance. She followed him inside.

Saima and her mother were inside, as well as the elderly healer, Qaunaq. She was revered for her knowledge of helping wounds heal, and soon Pitu would be asking for lessons from her. His role was to look after the spirits, but a shaman also needed to know how to heal.

Ijiraq was unconscious and feverish, his wounds covered in whale fat and mushed-up plants. Saima looked at them as they entered, her eyes red and watering. As she saw Ikuma, Saima said, "Welcome to our community."

Ikuma raised her brows at the polite greeting.

"You wanted to speak to me?" Pitu asked.

"Yes." Saima wiped the sleeve of her amauti against her nose, looking back down to Ijiraq. The other women in the iglu were quiet. Perhaps they should have been alone for this conversation. Pitu didn't know what Saima wanted to say to him. She looked back at Ikuma before finally resting her gaze on Pitu. "We don't know if Ijiraq will survive."

Pitu didn't want to admit that the spirits didn't know either. He moved farther into the iglu, making his way next to Saima and Ijiraq. His friend took deep, rattling breaths. Pitu said, "Your husband and I grew very close over the past few weeks."

Saima gave him a small smile, wistfully saying, "You two are very similar."

Pitu could feel it. A mutual desire to hold hands, to embrace one another. He looked away, back to Ikuma.

"Please, Piturniq," Saima murmured, averting her eyes back to Ijiraq's body. She took hold of her husband's hand. "Ask the spirits to help. Ask them to keep him strong and to heal his wounds."

"Of course," Pitu said. "I will do everything I can to help."

He reached over to touch the top of Ijiraq's head, feeling through his fingertips the pain of those wounds. Ijiraq's breaths slowed, his fever cooling slightly. He took his hand away, willing the alleviation to last until the next day. Pitu didn't know if it would work, but he hoped he could speak to Tiri before Ijiraq's brief calm wore off.

Saima let go of Ijiraq's hand, turning her focus back to Ikuma. She approached the other girl. For a moment, Pitu was scared of what she might do, but Saima only reached out to hug Ikuma. They embraced each other, tears falling from their eyes. He could hear Saima whispering praise into Ikuma's hair, proud of her bravery in speaking in front of a qaggiq full of strangers, in telling her story. Ikuma whimpered with each word of support. When they let go, Saima said again, "I am happy you've come."

"I am, too," Ikuma replied.

Afterward, Pitu held Ikuma's hand as they walked back to his mother's. She would be staying with Anaana for the time being. He said goodnight, and she went inside.

Pitu walked the short distance to his iglu, still standing, though it hadn't been occupied in weeks. His dog team surrounded the iglu, curled into sleeping balls. Miki lifted a dozing head in greeting, but for the first time, the husky didn't rise to rub her head against his approaching legs.

Atiq and Natsivaq had unloaded Pitu's supplies from the trip. They had cleaned Ijiraq's blood from the qamutiik, then flipped it. Natsivaq had also taken Pitu's blood-covered caribou furs away to be cleaned, replacing them with new ones.

He went inside. It seemed that Natsivaq had also kept the iglu in shape, making sure to light a qulliq inside for a while each day to ensure the layer of melted snow and ice remained to keep the integrity of the iglu strong. Pitu lit his qulliq, unrolled the new caribou skins, and lay them flat on the hard-packed sleeping area. He took the fox furs from their wrap of sealskin, laying them upon the bed.

Pitu didn't know if he had done the right thing, if he should have made his decision in private, if he should have punished Qajaarjuaq more and not shamed Tagaaq in front of their whole village. At the time, it had felt like the right thing to do, but now . . .

A woman entered Pitu's iglu then. *Who could be coming in?* he thought. He was shocked and didn't know what to do.

It was someone Pitu recognized, but he couldn't quite remember where he knew her from. He was stunned by her beauty, her skin tanned as if she'd just been under the summer sun. Two braids framed her face, looped to the back of her head, and melted into the rest of her long brown hair. She wore a caribou parka that was different from anyone in his village, the length of it reaching from her head to her ankles. She was from the west.

A memory sprang up. He knew that she was not just any woman. She was the spirit of a shaman, once sent to this camp to reprimand Pitu for not heeding Nuliajuk's invitation more quickly. He knew more about her now. He knew that she had cut Nuliajuk's hair, just as he had.

"Ai," Pitu said, not knowing what else to say.

"*Piturniq,*" the woman said, her voice just as powerful and otherworldly as it had been the first time she'd spoken to him, "*I've come to bring you another warning.*"

He waited quietly, not just out of politeness, but out of exhaustion. *Another warning so soon?*

"*You've completed your task,*" she said. "*But you've set up a new one. You did not listen to the advice to be careful of the company you kept on your journey. Prepare, young Piturniq. Prepare for what comes next. That hunter is not going to live out the rest of his life in quiet solitude. Prepare for what he will do next.*"

She left then, in a burst of cold wind.

Pitu sighed. Another warning for another day. For now, he was too tired, and it didn't sound urgent. He decided to prepare by lying down on the bed and waiting for his body heat and the fire of the qulliq to heat the iglu and warm the caribou skins. As he grew warmer, he slowly undressed. Pitu touched the fox-bone necklace he wore, calling Tiri. She appeared, and they spoke until Pitu fell asleep.

Glossary

-ngai		Suffix, endearment term
Aasivak	[aa-si-vak]	Name meaning "spider"
ai	[a-i]	Greeting
ainngai	[a-i-nga-i]	Affectionate greeting
Alaralak	[a-la-ra-lak]	Name
Amarualik	[a-ma-ru-a-lik]	Name
amauti	[a-ma-u-ti]	Woman's parka with large hood for carrying babies
anaana	[a-naa-na]	Mother
angakkuq	[a-ngak-kooq]	Shaman
Angugaattiaq	[a-ngu-gaat-ti-aq]	Name
angunasuktialuk	[a-ngu-na-suk-ti-a-look]	Great hunter
Aqiggiq	[a-qig-giq]	Name meaning "ptarmigan"
Arnaapik	[ar-naa-pik]	Name
atii	[a-tee]	"Come on"; "Let's go"
Atiq	[a-tiq]	Name
avani	[a-va-ni]	"Over there" or "Go away"
Hiiguuq?	[hee-gooq]	"Really?"
iggaak	[ig-gaak]	Sunglasses made from bone
iglu	[ig-lu]	Dome-shaped house made of snow

igluit	[ig-lu-eet]	Plural of "iglu"
Iilaak	[ii-laak]	"I know"
Ijiraq	[i-ji-raq]	Name; also a creature in Inuit legends that is a shapeshifter or very thin and hard to see
ikajuqtaulanga	[i-ka-yooq-ta-u-la-nga]	"Help me"
Ikuma	[i-ku-ma]	Name meaning "fire"
Inukpak	[i-nuk-pak]	Giant
Inuuja	[i-nuu-ya]	Name meaning "doll"
Ivalu	[i-va-lu]	Name meaning "sinew/thread"
Ka'lak	[ka'-lak]	Name
kamiik	[ka-meek]	Pair of boots
kanajuit	[ka-na-yuit]	Rock fish; sculpins
kanajuq	[ka-na-yooq]	One sculpin
katuut	[ka-tuut]	Drum beater
Kinauvit	[ki-na-u-vit]	"Who are you?" "What's your name?"
Kiviuq	[ki-vi-uq]	A legendary Inuk traveller
kunik	[ku-nik]	An Inuit version of a kiss: placing one's nose on another's cheek and inhaling
Mahaha	[ma-ha-ha]	A creature that tickles its victims to death
maktaaq	[mak-taaq]	Beluga or narwhal skin with blubber
Miki	[mi-ki]	Name meaning "small."

Nagliktaujuit	[nag-li-ta-u-yoot]	Abused people's lives taken by a spirit
Nagliktaujuq	[nag-lik-ta-u-yooq]	Abused person's life taken by a spirit
Nagliktaujut Nunangat	[nag-lik-ta-u-yoot nu-na-ngat]	Land of the abused people's lives taken by spirits
nanuq	[na-nuq]	Polar bear
Nassak	[nas-sak]	Name
Natsivaq	[nat-si-vak]	Name
Nuliajuk	[nu-li-a-yuk]	A well-known sea spirit that lives at the bottom of the ocean and controls sea animals.
nunangat	[nu-na-ngat]	Homeland
Nuvuk	[nu-vuk]	Common place name, referring to a point of land
pana	[pa-na]	Snow knife used for making an iglu
Panninguaq	[pan-ni-ngu-aq]	Name
pissi	[pis-si]	Dried fish
Piturniirngai	[pi-toor-neer-nga-i]	"Hi, Piturniq"
Piturniq	[pi-toor-niq]	Name meaning "time of high tide caused by the full moon"
puukuluk	[puu-ku-luk]	Biological mother
qaggiq	[qag-giq]	A giant iglu made for celebration purposes, as well as the celebration for the return of the sun
qajaarjuaq	[qa-jaar-ju-aq]	Name
qajaq	[qa-yaq]	Kayak

qallupilluit	[qal-lu-pil-lu-it]	Creatures that live in the ocean and steal children
qamutiik	[qa-mu-teek]	Sled
qamutiit	[qa-mu-teet]	Sleds
Qanuinnavit	[qa-nu-in-na-vit]	"What's wrong?"
Qujannamiik	[qu-yan-na-meek]	"Thank you"
qulliit	[qul-liit]	Seal-oil lamps
qupanuaq	[qu-pa-nu-aq]	Snow bunting
Saimaniq	[sa-i-ma-niq]	Name meaning "peace"
sila	[si-la]	Sky, environment, air, weather
silattiaq	[si-lat-ti-aq]	Beautiful weather
Tagaaq	[ta-gaaq]	Name
Taktuq	[tak-tooq]	Name
Tiri	[ti-ri]	Name, short for tiriganniaq (fox)
Tumma	[tum-ma]	Name
tuurngaq	[tuur-ngaq]	Spirit
Ujarasuk	[u-ya-ra-sook]	Name
ukpik	[ook-pik]	Owl
Ullaakkut	[ul-laak-koot]	"Good morning"
uvanga	[u-va-nga]	Me
Uvangattauq	[u-va-ngat-ta-uq]	"Me too"

A note to readers: One sound in Inuktitut that might be more difficult for English speakers is the "ng" sound, which sounds like the "ng" in "sing."

Author's Note

I am a collection of languages, customs, and stories from across Inuit Nunangat, and this means that Pitu is, too. Though I grew up in Igloolik, my Inuktitut is a mixture of Nunavik and North Baffin dialects (this is why Pitu says "Ai" or "Anaanangai," which are typical in Nunavik, but not in Igloolik). In North Baffin, ijirait are monsters with distorted faces who live in rocks, but in the Kivalliq region, they are shapeshifters.

There are many different versions of the legend of Nuliajuk, and it has been a favourite of mine since childhood. Yes, I love her more than I love qallupilluit.

Inuit were (and still are) very frightened of Nuliajuk. If she was upset, she took away sea animals, and this meant starvation among many of our ancestral communities. Because we were so frightened of her, Inuit had many names to avoid saying her true name. In all the versions of her story, Nuliajuk is a young woman who refuses to get married, so her names often represented that. Many of the names also describe her as "the woman below," meaning the woman at the bottom of the ocean. She was known as Sanna (or, as it was anglicized, "Sedna"), Takkanaaluk, Sassuma Arnaa, Nerrivik, and many, many more names. She is also depicted in different ways, sometimes with a beluga tail, or as a large woman who sits very still at the bottom of the ocean, where any movement she makes could cause gigantic waves that could ruin coastal communities.

I consciously chose to depict Nuliajuk in the way I had always imagined her as I was growing up, with a fish tail, young and lonely at the bottom of the ocean. This may not be the typical representation of her, but that is who I saw when I heard her story, and that is who she is to me.

Acknowledgments

I would like to thank all of the amazing people who have been with me through this story. I don't know what I would do without Kelly Ward and Kathleen Keenan. They are fantastic editors, and I feel so taken care of when I work with them. Neil and Danny, thank you for all the opportunities and understanding, and letting me hang out with your families. I feel very lucky to work with a great company like Inhabit Media.

Qujannamiik to my colleagues at Nunavut Sivuniksavut. Your enthusiasm and encouragement for my writing career is truly appreciated.

Thank you again to all the beautiful Inuit who answered my questions about Inuit legends. It is always interesting to learn about the different versions of the same story from all over the different regions of our homeland.

Three ladies who should consider a career as harsh editors and critics are Marley Dunkers, Alianai Niviatsiak, and Zorga Qaunaq. Sometimes you guys hurt my feelings, but I love you.

As always, I have so much love for my friends Jackie, Todd, Aquack, Terrie, Robyn, and your babies and doggos. I am also thankful for all the friends I have made along the way.

I owe everything to my parents, Glen and Elisapee. They are so full of love and support, I am surprised it doesn't ooze out and stain their clothes.

Alannah and Tom, my sister and my brother, are cool people doing cool things and I am glad we are so close and that you guys are always with me every step of the way.

It has been humbling to have been met with such welcoming and praise in the literary community of Canada. It has been a privilege meeting fantastic writers and book lovers since *Those Who Run in the*

Sky came into this world. I hope that we all have good writing days in the future and that our paths cross again . . . and again and again.

INHABIT
M E D I A

Iqaluit · Toronto